THE
SOLDIER'S
GHOST

A Tale of Charleston

Karen Stokes

GREEN ALTAR BOOKS
Columbia, South Carolina

8-13-18

Published by Green Altar Books, an Imprint of

Shotwell Publishing, LLC
P.O. Box 2592
Columbia, South Carolina 29202

www.ShotwellPublishing.com

Cover image: *The Ghost Story* by R.W. Buss, 1874

SECOND EDITION

ISBN-13: 978-1947660144
ISBN-10: 1947660136

THE SOLDIER'S GHOST

B EFORE ALL THESE THINGS HAPPENED, I did not believe in ghosts. When I have told you my story, you may judge for yourself whether I have changed my mind.

My name is Mattie Campbell. I was christened Martha Rutledge Campbell, but I have always been called Mattie. I have a brother named Matthew, one year my junior, and when we were little, we were inseparable companions, Matt seldom being seen without his Mattie, and vice versa. We were born in South Carolina, in Charleston, and our father worked for a prosperous cotton merchant of that beautiful city. When the terrible war between the North and the South began in 1861, Papa joined the army, and life soon became so dangerous in Charleston that he sent us (Mama, Matt, me and our sister, Nannie) some sixty miles inland to live in a little pineland village called Summerton. An aunt who had a summer home there took us in as war refugees, and there we waited out the war in relative safety and comfort while Papa went off to Virginia to fight and endure many hardships.

Four years later, when it was all over, we were all unspeakably grateful that he came back to us. We stayed on at Summerton for a while and, in June 1865, Papa made a trip to Charleston to see how things were in the city and whether it would be safe for us to return. Much of the place was in shambles, he discovered, and there was no commerce to speak of. Wharves which had once bustled with shipping were a wasteland and, like almost all the other merchants of Charleston, the gentleman for whom Papa had worked for so many years was ruined as a businessman and could offer him no employment. When my father visited our house on Elizabeth Street, he found that it had been confiscated by the Yankee military authorities who were then all-powerful in the state. Though they soon returned the house to us, excepting some larger pieces of furniture, nearly everything of value had been stripped from it—even family portraits and photographs.

Mama wept bitterly when she walked through the familiar but now mostly empty rooms of our home again. The house had been damaged little by the shelling during the war—yet the whole place had a forlorn, faded look, and all its surrounding gardens, once so carefully tended   and   cultivated,   were   wild-looking   and overgrown.

My father could find no work, and no way to support us. Mama was forced to part with her jewelry, silverware, and a few other valuables she had managed to preserve and, piece by piece, she sold them to keep us from starvation. Then one day in early September, news came that a first cousin had died and left Papa a farm in an area called Charleston Neck, a few miles north of the city. Our Uncle Pink (whose proper name was Pinckney Brewton) had lived there for many years, until he passed away during the war. His son, Pinckney Jr., inherited the land, but severe wounds he received in military service brought about his early death, and so the property became ours. It was called Brewton Farm; we all knew the place well and loved it. It had come to Uncle Pink through his wife's family, having once been part of a much larger tract on the wider part of the "neck" owned by his father-in-law. Rice had once been grown on some of the original lands, but our property was not suitable for that crop, having no marshland or creeks. There was a large house there, many acres of good farm and forest land, and an orchard stocked with apple, pear and other fruit-bearing trees. My father decided that we would move to Brewton Farm where he could work the land and, at least, provide food for his family. Charleston was so full of Yankee soldiers and carpetbaggers, he wasn't sorry to leave it.

It was at the farm that I first heard of the ghost—a soldier's ghost—said to haunt the nearby woods and fields.

* * *

When we arrived at Brewton Farm one September morning, I found that the two-story house there was much as I remembered it, except that its white paint was now worn and peeling, and like our house in Charleston it wore the same forlorn, abandoned look, having had little care or improvement for several years. One of the largest outbuildings on the farm was a barn, a large, handsome structure of white clapboard and, in the center of its high roof, there was a cupola topped by a weathervane.

We discovered that most of the servants who had lived and worked at the farm for years had gone off or died. Only the old cook, Bess, remained and it was from her that Matthew and I first heard of the ghost inhabiting the place. On our first night at the farm, after we had claimed our rooms and put away the few belongings we brought, we left our new home and walked the short path to the kitchen house to see her. She was making supper, fashioning some biscuit dough with her gnarled brown hands, and when we came in, she immediately put us to work, too. As we helped her, she informed us that something downright peculiar had been going on at the farm since wintertime. A ghost, she said, had come to haunt the place. She told us that it wore a uniform of gray, and that it was the ghost of a soldier. She had seen it once herself, and other servants had caught glimpses of it from time to time and heard its eerie, unearthly groans and mutterings in the night.

Matthew believed what old Bess told us, his attitude being that the existence of ghosts was not a matter to dispute. I, on the other hand, was very skeptical and rather proudly so. Though I did not say it, it was my opinion that it was only the simple, uneducated, or superstitious among us who believed in such things. Matthew was still just a boy, and I expected him to grow out of such childish fantasies, just as I had.

I was nearly seventeen when we took up residence at Brewton Farm, and considered myself no longer a little girl but a young lady. As a child of course, I had believed in all sorts of fanciful things, from fairies to goblins. Once, a cousin had given me a little collection of gothic novels and, for a while, I was delighted by these frightening, thrilling tales which, knowing that my parents would disapprove of such sensational literature, I read in secrecy. When I was about twelve, I remember reading a ghost story by Mrs. Gaskell by candlelight one evening, and though I found it very entertaining, my heart skipped a beat when I heard a strange sound very close by. I was alone in my room, or so I thought, and as the sounds continued, I began to feel quite certain, and quite terrified, that something, some kind of phantom, was in my bed chamber with me. As it turned out, it was only my cat, playing with some ribbon she had found on the floor, and this made me feel very silly indeed. After that I put away such books, and such foolish fancies, and found other things to read.

Besides old Bess, the only other inhabitant of the farm before our arrival was our cousin, Isham, Uncle Pink's only surviving son. When Papa inherited the farm, he also inherited the responsibility for this poor, helpless creature—a thin, gangling, sometimes sickly, and somewhat deranged young man who was about twenty-five years of age. Kindly people called him simpleminded; others who were not so kind said he was just plain crazy. For years, Uncle Pink considered sending him to live at the state lunatic asylum in Columbia, and had vacillated about it for a long time, but when one of his other sons died in battle during the war, he found he could not part with his youngest, and kept Isham with him.

Our cousin Isham was homely, and looked a little strange, but he was harmless. Sometimes he acted very strangely; one day, I saw him take off his hat, place it on the ground, and walk around it three times before he picked it up and put it back on his head. Papa was with me at the time, and I asked him what Isham was doing.

"I questioned the boy about that once," said my

father, "and he told me that God had instructed him to walk around his hat whenever he felt himself in trouble or danger, and that doing this would afford him protection."

"Do you really think God told him that?" I wondered aloud. "It's a very odd notion."

Papa smiled and said, "Whether he did or not, as long as it gives the boy comfort, I see nothing wrong with it."

Isham was not very strong, but he was capable of doing simple work around the farm. He liked to help my father on wash days, and even seemed to enjoy this long, tedious chore, making a game of it somehow. Papa would not allow any of us to help him with the washing of clothes and linens except Isham or Matthew. He had taken on this work in Charleston, and continued it at the farm, because he could not bear the thought of our mother doing it.

"My wife is a lady," he had declared to us. "She will not perform drudgery. I will not have it."

It amazed us all, but he was true to his word, and my mother never did do the washing. One day a week was set aside for this task, and all the other days of the week, except Sunday, my father worked in the fields.

When Papa made an inspection of the farm on our first day of residence, he found that some of the boards had been torn away from the side of the big barn, leaving a gaping hole in one of its walls. Someone had taken the wood to use for another purpose, and there were also many parts of fences which had been taken down.

It was nearly autumn when we left Charleston for our new home on the neck, and by that time it was too late to plant corn, but Mama sold off the last of the family valuables and with the money we purchased just enough supplies, seed, feed and livestock to see us through the winter. Having been born and raised on a plantation, my father knew a great deal about agriculture, and immediately set about putting all the outbuildings, fences and implements in good repair and preparing the fields for a few winter crops and spring planting. Papa had been a well-dressed, clean shaven man of business before; now he looked exactly like a farmer. He came back from the war with a full beard, and kept it. I didn't like the beard, because I thought my father had a handsome face, and now it was hidden.

My first and most important responsibility on the farm was the poultry. Our chickens provided eggs and meat, which were sometimes sold or bartered for other necessities. The physician and apothecary were often paid for their services with this type of currency. The hen-house was my domain, the hens and chicks and roosters my fussy little subjects; the eggs, my treasury.

Besides the chickens, there was only one other

feathered creature that belonged to the farm. Being fond of peacocks, Uncle Pink had owned a small flock of these beautiful creatures, but we found none of them on our arrival at Brewton Farm. They were all gone—or so we thought, and then, on the first day of November, a single white peacock meandered into the farmyard and, afterward, stayed within sight of the house most days. When he fanned out his tail to display it, we saw that some of the larger feathers were missing or broken. Papa named him Ichabod.

* * *

I think most gentlemen would not have considered my mother beautiful, but she was to all who loved her, especially Papa. She had honey-colored hair and a long, delicate face, serene and gentle in expression. Hers was a spiritual rather than a physical beauty. Our cook Bess often had spells of illness or weakness, and Mama, who had only supervised the preparation of meals before, took on much of the cooking and kitchen work herself, and learned to be a very good cook indeed. All of us, except Papa, knew that she was making most of the meals for the family table. She asked us not to tell him, but I think he eventually began to have his suspicions.

Mama also learned to mend and sew our clothes. She had always been clever with her hands but, in the past, her needlework had been only in the nature of a genteel lady's pastime resulting in decorative embroideries and lace. Now she made us dresses and shirts and pantaloons, and knitted socks and other garments. Papa didn't seem to mind seeing her at her sewing; it was a sedate and ladylike activity; and though he himself constantly toiled like a field hand, he could not bear to think of her engaging in any kind of strenuous labor. He kept a watchful eye on her, and would gently scold her if he thought she was overexerting herself in any way.

Before the war, Mama had done some gardening, but only to amuse herself by the cultivation of ornamental plants and flowers. Now, out of necessity, she turned her attention to vegetables. She consulted an old almanac and a book on gardening that she had purchased for a trifling sum, and with their direction, and some advice from knowledgeable acquaintances, she planted a kitchen garden. Under her supervision, Isham did the digging, and he and I helped with the weeding after the seeds were planted. I also pulled off the insect pests and fed them to my chickens.

In the evenings, Mama would confer with Papa about her gardening plans.

"The gardener's calendar says that turnips may be sowed at the full of the moon in August," she informed him, holding the little book to read by the light of a tallow candle. "Oh, dear, I suppose it is too late to sow them now it is September."

"Yes, I think it is too late for that," Papa opined. "Besides, we haven't any seed."

"Well, then, for September, the ground may be prepared for spinach, lettuce, and radishes," said Mama.

"I'll try to get you some seed for those," Papa offered, though he looked doubtful about the prospect. We had precious little money left to buy such things.

It worried Mama that my brother and I were receiving no formal education while we lived at the farm. After we left Summerton, our schooling became sporadic. Our mother tried to find time to continue our instruction, teaching us lessons here and there, and quizzing us during meals, but everyone was so busy with farm and house work that there was little time for anything else.

When we were very young, Matthew and I attended separate academies in Charleston. In Summerton, Mama tried to take on the part of tutor, but she had so many other responsibilities, she soon turned us over to a professional teacher, a crippled man whose twisted legs had kept him out of military service. He walked with a peculiar lurch, and was quite ugly, but he was gentle and kind, and a good teacher. He tutored us and several other children of refugee families, instructing his pupils in Latin, geometry, literature, and many other subjects. He once told my mother that I was his best scholar, and that I even excelled in mathematics.

Matthew did tolerably well, but he was not of a scholarly nature. My brother preferred energetic play and even work to schooling. In Summerton, and at the farm, he never complained when he was asked to cut firewood or help with chores that required male strength; I think it made him feel manly.

* * *

My sister Anne, called Nannie, helped Mama as much as she could with the housework and cooking at the farm, but much of her time and energy was devoted to the care of her baby. At the age of twenty-one, she was already a widow.

During the war, Nannie became engaged to a gallant, handsome Confederate officer, and I will always treasure their bittersweet romance as one of the most beautiful memories of my girlhood. His name was Micah Johnson. He was a distant cousin, and a neighbor in Charleston, and I think he loved my sister all his life. He was four years older than Nannie, and on her seventeenth birthday, he asked my father for her hand in marriage. Papa said she was too young, and told Micah he might ask for her again in a year's time. During the year he had to wait, the war began, and in the summer of 1861 he went off to Virginia with his regiment. In the first great battle at Manassas, he and many other South Carolinians distinguished themselves in a great victory and were all welcomed home as heroes.

I shall never forget the day Micah returned to Charleston after that battle. After seeing his family he came to visit us, of course, dressed in a fine new uniform, and newly promoted to the rank of captain. I thought him even handsomer than before. He looked more like a man now, not a boy, and had grown a dark mustache. It was the same color as his thick, dark brown hair, which was carefully arranged with short sideburns that curled up just a little at the top, just above his fine eyebrows and dark blue eyes. His figure was strong and straight, his manners those of a gentleman, and I thought him the perfect picture of chivalry. I was only about thirteen then, and in my girlish romanticism, I loved him madly, and considered my sister the most fortunate woman in the world.

One fair, cool October evening, we all had supper together, and I managed to secure a seat next to Micah, and even dared to slip my arm around his a few times as we talked and joked. Knowing my penchant for reading, and my reputation as a scholar, he called me "professor" and asked me questions that allowed me to show off my learning. My warlike little brother, who was already itching to be a soldier, he addressed as "captain," and instructed him on how to go about commanding his men on the battlefield. Oh, how we ate up such flattery, facetious as it was. He was so charming! Even my father admired him and fell under his spell, and was soon persuaded to reconsider the postponement of his engagement to Nannie.

Later that evening, Matthew and I were sent to our rooms so that the grown-ups could converse without the benefit of our antics. I was wanting a new book to read, and before going upstairs, I took a candle into Papa's study to find one. I spent some time looking through several interesting new volumes full of colorful pictures, and when I had settled on one for myself, I noticed how the room was full of moonlight. A full moon had just risen and was shining in with all its might, drawing me to the window. I opened it, and felt a gentle cool breeze wafting in as I looked up to admire the beauty of the lesser light.

The window looked out into our garden, and I had not been standing there long when I heard familiar voices and footsteps close by. I blew out the candle and drew back a bit, the voices growing more distinct, until I could see Micah and Nannie slowly strolling along together down a graveled path. They were walking together alone—unchaperoned! This could only mean they were engaged now. I was so happy, I could have danced a jig, but I kept myself very still and quiet.

Micah asked my sister for a kiss, and she consented. I don't think they had ever kissed before—certainly not the way they kissed that night. Was there ever such a kiss I thought, swooning as if I had been the one in his arms.

When it was over I heard him say to her, "My heart hasn't beat so fast since I was being shot at."

"Oh, Micah," my sister sighed, turning her head. "Please don't speak of such things."

He murmured something apologetic, and she turned back to him with a smile. He was still holding her, hoping for another kiss, which soon followed. They began to speak of wedding plans, and walked on, until I could no longer hear their conversation.

Within two months, the two lovers were married, and a little over two years after that, our dear gallant Micah fell in battle and died within hours. Nannie was expecting at the time, and though heartbroken by her loss, a few months later she had the consolation of a little baby boy we all adored. He was a beautiful child, and it was no wonder, for his father was a very handsome man—the handsomest I ever saw—and his mother had the face of an angel.

Nannie lived with us in Summerton, and was still with us when we moved back to Charleston. Just after we went to reside at Brewton Farm, an old family friend came to call on us, a young planter named Charles Mouzon who had once courted Nannie, and still loved her. Like nearly everyone else in the state, he had lost much of his fortune because of the war, but he had some money and property abroad, and was intending to leave the country and settle in Canada.

After several visits, he asked Nannie to be his wife and go away with him, and she said yes. One night I overheard Mr. Mouzon speaking to my father, who was already grieving the loss of his daughter and grandson, assuring him of his great love for Nannie, and promising to do everything in his power to make her happy.

"It isn't every man who obtains the idol and dream of his heart," I heard him say to Papa. "I will take care of her, Mr. Campbell, and love the child as if he were my own."

A few days after Nannie was married, on the eve of her departure, she came to the house to say her goodbyes to us. Everyone was sad to part with her, and our darling baby boy, but I felt that I was the one most to be pitied. Nannie and I had always been so devoted to each other, so close, such good friends—I thought my heart would break to lose her.

That evening Matthew manfully controlled his feelings in order not to cry, and Papa also remained composed, though I could tell that he was suffering. Mama held the baby, kissing him repeatedly and periodically sniffing and blinking back tears. I wept openly, however, and held on to my sister's arm and hand as much as I could.

Seeing me so inconsolable, Nannie sweetly suggested that she and I have a private conversation, and we went up to my room, where we sat together on the bed and talked as we had so many times before. We reminisced about our years in Summerton, and some adventures we shared there.

"Do you remember the camp meetings?" she asked, smiling mischievously.

"Oh, dear!" I cried, laughing despite my tears. "I can never forget those!"

One October, just outside Summerton, people from all around the area came in wagons and buggies and on foot to gather in a field for religious services that lasted nearly a week. Most of them set up tents to live in for the duration of the meeting, bringing their own food and drink. There were nearly two hundred people assembled there, fully half of whom were negroes, the latter attired in their best, most colorful clothing. The preachers were Methodists, but I think the attendees represented a number of denominations. Nannie and I wanted to go to the camp meeting on its opening day just for diversion, eager for a break in the dull routine of country life. Mama, knowing how Papa disapproved of the religious excitement that characterized such affairs, hesitated about giving us permission, but after much begging from us she finally gave in. We left the house on a Thursday afternoon, and walked to the camp grounds in the company of some neighbors. One of these was a young lady of Nannie's age, Miss Ashe , and another,

Emmeline Marineau, was a girl just a little older than me. Like us, they were refugees from Charleston, and we were all good friends.

The first service began at dusk, and a preacher from Virginia surprised us with a splendid sermon. That night we saw little of religious excitement, and after the preaching everyone enjoyed supper at their tents or in the chairs set up for the congregation. It was more like a picnic than a camp meeting. Everyone seemed to be enjoying themselves immensely, and among the young people there was some courting and flirting going on. We enjoyed ourselves, too, and determined to come back the next morning and bring along a picnic lunch.

The following day, however, things took a more serious turn at the evening service. A fiery minister from Georgia, who was traveling all over the country collecting money to publish Bible tracts for the soldiers, preached a fervent, stirring sermon that caused some of the hearers to cry out or break into convulsions called the jerks. As he thundered on, others in the congregation fell down as if struck dead, and among the negroes, there was shouting, clapping, swaying, and laughing of the "holy laugh."

Witnessing all this, Nannie and I understood what Papa meant by religious excitement. Accustomed to the orderly, formal worship of our Presbyterian church in Charleston, and the stately, intellectual sermons of our minister Rev. Dr. Thomson, we were somewhat bewildered and even a little alarmed by these outlandish emotional demonstrations. Miss Marineau, an Episcopalian, was really quite frightened.

"Emmie did not go back after that!" my sister recalled laughingly.

"But you and I were brave enough to return on Saturday," I said. "And that's when the soldier proposed to you!"

"I ought to have been nicer to him," Nannie mused. "But it he was very impertinent."

One afternoon at the camp meeting, a handsome young soldier on furlough came up to Nannie and said that he had been given a "special revelation" by the Lord that they were to be married. My sister's blithe reply to him that day was, "When the Lord gives me the same revelation, I will let you know."

"I don't think he had any such revelation," I laughed, falling back on the pillows of my bed. "But you were the prettiest young lady at the meeting, and I suppose he thought he would try his luck. He did laugh as you and I walked away."

"Yes, but he ought to have been more reverent," said Nannie. "Still, he was a soldier, and I should have just told him that I was already married."

We talked and laughed about a few more amusing incidents that happened at the camp meeting, and

brought up other memories of our time in Summerton,
but when Nannie mentioned her husband Micah, I
began to cry again. My sister put her arms around me
and offered me the comforting reminder that we would
see him again someday. As I took deep breaths to calm
myself, she said soothingly, "I know that you miss him,
Mattie. I miss him, too, so very much. But a part of him
is still with us, isn't he? And now our little Micah will
have a new father, and Charles and I will watch him
grow up, and you will see him, too. I shall write to you
regularly and send you his photograph, and ours, and
when you are older, you must come and visit us."

"Oh! I should like that!" I said, brightening. I had
never traveled anywhere faraway.

"You will write to me, won't you, Mattie?" she
asked.

"Every month!" I promised. "Every week, if
possible."

* * *

Uncle Pink was a strange old bird, Mama always
said of him—fondly, though, for she had loved him very
much. He had been a lawyer for many years, and it was
rumored that he had accumulated a great deal of money,
but if he did, no Charleston banker ever saw much of it,
and no one would have guessed him for a rich man from
his modest, even miserly style of living. Just after the
death of his wife, he retired from the practice of law, sold

his town house in Charleston, and took up permanent residence at his farm. Though somewhat eccentric, he was clever in many ways, and very learned, and one of the few luxuries he allowed himself was a fine library. He was also a student of history, and had collected many old letters and documents from various relatives. These were the papers of our ancestors, one of whom had been a rather significant personage of the Revolution. Perhaps fearing that these valuable manuscripts might be lost someday, Uncle Pink wrote out copies of all or most of them, painstakingly transcribing them in his remarkably neat, elegant handwriting that resembled calligraphy.

Like many places in the state, Brewton Farm had been pillaged during the war. We found that many things were missing from the house, and Papa was especially disappointed that Uncle Pink's important papers were nowhere to be found—until one day, when we happened upon them quite by accident. On that same day, we also discovered what I considered an equally valuable and delightful treasure—a library.

One of the few books we had at the farm was *Les Miserables* by Mr. Hugo. Someone had sent it to Papa while he was a prisoner of war, and my brother I took turns with it until it was nearly falling apart. I loved this story of redemption, and marveled at the kind priest who was so merciful toward a rough, uncouth convict, and thus revived his conscience, faith and humanity.

Most of all, though, being a romantic girl, I reveled in the love story of Marius and Cosette, sighing over the beautiful, lyrical descriptions of their great devotion. I enjoyed reading the novel again, but I longed for more books, and quite unexpectedly, my wish was granted.

One day, I heard some hammering going on in the room which had once been Uncle Pink's library. I went in and found that Papa had removed some of the book shelves, and was beginning to pound away under the edge of a large wooden window seat. He was going to make some furniture Mama needed, he said, and was taking some of the wood from this room, which looked to be fine, sturdy oak. Empty as they were, I hated to see a gaping, even emptier space in the book shelves, about three or four of which were now piled on the floor, but I was suddenly and unexpectedly consoled when I heard Papa exclaim, "Well, I'll be!"

He had removed the top part of the window seat, and was looking down into what lay beneath it as if gazing into a treasure chest. And what a treasure it was! It was filled with books. I squealed with delight, and Papa took time from his work to help me bring out and examine all our newfound prizes.

"Uncle Pink must have hidden these here," he told me. "I wondered why the seat was nailed shut. I remember hiding in it when I was a boy."

Under some of the books we found several boxes

and bundles of paper tied with ribbons, and Papa breathed a sigh of relief when he saw them. These were the family papers Uncle Pink had preserved.

"I'll look at these later," said Papa, carefully lifting them out and placing them on a table.

Beneath the papers were still more books, and my father returned to the window seat to help me remove them. Both of us sat on the floor for close to half an hour looking through all the titles, Papa allowing himself this pleasant little interlude. Those titles I considered to be the dullest and least interesting, such as theologies and books about English law, were the ones Papa selected for himself, informing me that they had belonged to his grandfather. More interesting to me were books about ancient history, some of which were written in Latin.

"Matthew will like these," I said to Papa. "He has learned his Latin."

My father received this pronouncement with a half-smiling grimace of skepticism, but he then smiled very broadly as he pulled out another book from our trove, knowing that it would please me. It was Dickens! Glorious, beloved Dickens. *A Tale of Two Cities* met my eyes, and even better, it was one of his works which I had not yet devoured.

"A good story," Papa remarked drily. "But I will let you have it to enjoy. I have had enough of Jacobins."

He reached into the window seat again and, still

smiling, pulled out two more Dickens gems for me, *David Copperfield,* and *A Christmas Carol.*

"A Christmas Carol!" I cried. "We must save that for Christmas, Papa. We must read it aloud on Christmas eve."

Papa thought this was a very good idea. There followed a few more novels to my taste by Sir Walter Scott and William Gilmore Simms, volumes of Shakespeare and Homer, and histories of our Revolution, along with a wealth of other reading material that made me giddy with anticipation.

"Oh, Papa," I exulted. "How I shall love to sit here in the window and read all of these books!"

He turned his gaze to the window seat thoughtfully, and after a moment said to me, "I did that myself sometimes as a boy. I ought not to take it away from you."

"Oh, no, Papa!" I protested. "You must take the wood if you need it."

"No, no," he said, shaking his head. "I can find something else. I shall leave it as it is."

I thanked him and hugged his neck, saying how I could hardly wait.

"You mustn't neglect your chores, Mattie," he admonished me, seeing my elation. "I know you are a bookworm, but work must come first now. You may read in the evenings when your work is done."

And so I did. I read each night until my weary eyelids grew too heavy to keep open, and devoured many a book on Sunday afternoons after church, cozy in my window seat (my Sabbath readings being histories and biographies). Sometimes, my brother would join me in the window seat; it was large enough for two, and there so many books in it that we never had to fight over one. Our mother was glad to see us reading so much.

In the evenings, I liked to read aloud for my family, and they seemed to enjoy it. Mama would usually sew while she listened, but Papa was always so tired from a long day's work that he often fell asleep in his chair before I finished a chapter. Isham seemed to listen very intently to anything I read, but I don't know how much of it he comprehended or remembered.

I know that there was one particular thing I read that did impress our cousin's strange, addled brain very much for some reason, and it apparently remained a concern in his mind for some time afterward. I was reading chapter fourteen of *David Copperfield,* and the part that dealt with one certain character seemed to elicit Isham's special attention. I think Isham might have detected a kindred spirit in the amiable madman named Mr. Dick, who believed that when the head of King Charles I was cut off many centuries ago, some of the trouble from it was somehow put into Mr. Dick's head.

For several days after the reading of this part of the

novel, something seemed to be worrying Isham. It was quite unusual, for he was usually quite thoughtless and carefree in his simplemindedness. We noticed him walking around his hat several times, and one day, very curious about his preoccupation, Matthew and I asked him what was wrong. Isham was reluctant to tell us at first, but when we had pestered him enough, he finally made a confession.

Looking deeply serious and concerned, he said to us, "I don't want that trouble in King Charles' head getting into mine."

Instantly, my brother and I burst into helpless laughter; we couldn't help it. It was too funny to bear. Isham looked very hurt by our mirth, and tears began to roll down his cheeks. It was the first and only time I ever saw him cry. We tried to sober ourselves, but could not stop laughing, and Isham ran away and hid himself from us.

When we recovered some composure, Matthew and I were heartily ashamed of ourselves for having wounded the feelings of our poor, feebleminded cousin. We looked for him all over the farm, intending to apologize for our bad behavior, and while we searched, the two of us also came up with a way to help Isham with his problem. After hunting for him for nearly an hour, we walked out to the family cemetery near the edge of the woods. The long, sturdy limbs of an enormous, ancient live oak tree spread out over most of the graves, and in the shadiest spot, we finally found Isham, concealed and whimpering behind the big, rectangular, ivy-covered tomb of our great, great grandfather.

His homely face was very sad, and his eyes were red from weeping.

"Please forgive us, cousin," I said, kneeling on the ground in front of him. "We weren't laughing at you, you know."

"You were!" he wailed.

"No, no, Isham!" I insisted. "We were laughing because what you fear is impossible! Quite impossible."

His brow contracted in dull puzzlement.

"It's impossible, you see," I went on, "because King Charles was an English king, and could only bother Englishmen. You are an American, so he cannot possibly trouble you."

Isham blinked several times, his eyes rolling around a little with the thoughts turning over in his head, and at last answered wonderingly, "I clean forgot that."

"No need to worry about it anymore, my good man," Matt declared with great authority in his voice, standing over us. "The idea is utterly ridiculous."

Isham smiled and sighed in relief. After that, King Charles never bothered our cousin again.

* * *

One day a visitor came to the farm asking for Adam Campbell. Adam was my father's brother, and the visitor was a friend who served with him during the war. My father had to inform him that Adam was in all likelihood dead, for we had not heard from him for nearly a year. When the visitor left, my father went off by himself, and I believe I heard him sobbing as he closed the door of the library behind him. The loss of this beloved brother was one of his greatest sorrows.

Uncle Adam had served bravely throughout the war, and had been wounded several times, once very seriously. He had also spent time in the hands of the enemy before being exchanged as a prisoner of war. Each time he was wounded, after a convalescence at home or in a hospital, he had gone right back into the army. He fought in many battles in Virginia, and was stationed in Charleston for a while, but Papa lost touch with him in early 1865, all our letters to him going unanswered after that time. When the end of the war came, and many more months passed with no news of him or from him, we reluctantly and sadly gave him up for dead. Later, someone told Papa that he heard that Adam had died at the battle of Bentonville in North Carolina, but we never had any official confirmation of his fate. We knew of other families with similar stories to tell of lost loved ones. Such things happen in war.

Papa would sometimes take out a small photograph of Adam and gaze at it. I would sit in his lap and gaze at it, too. He was a handsome young man, a favorite in our family. He had a sweet disposition and face, though in this little photographic portrait, dressed in a uniform, he was somewhat frowning and even a little fierce-looking as he held up the lethal blade of a large Bowie knife. He was about fifteen years younger than my father—a half-brother, in fact, being the only child of my grandfather's second marriage.

* * *

In early November, a stranger purchased a farm that bordered ours and took up residence there. Like most people we knew, the family who had owned this land for many years had fallen on hard times and could not keep it up, nor pay the taxes on it. Its owner, a widow, had lost three sons in the war, as well as her husband, and was going off somewhere to live with a married daughter.

We found out quickly enough that the new owner was a northerner, and that he had leased the property to a former officer in the Yankee army. There were a number of such men in the state at that time, and for many years afterward, and they were the principal ones who had money to buy land and establish businesses. Papa was highly displeased about our new neighbor, but being a Christian man, he resolved to at least show himself neighborly to a reasonable degree (though it irked him, I could tell).

My father was a deacon of our church, and when regular services resumed in the late summer of 1865, we would travel a number of miles down the neck into the city of Charleston each Sunday in our carriage to join with the remnants of our old congregation. Our pastor, Rev. Dr. Thomson, though not extremely elderly, was in poor health, and Papa would assist him in any way that he could. Though many of our members were still scattered elsewhere as refugees of war, little by little they returned to Charleston, almost all of them, like the church itself, having been reduced to poverty.

One Sunday morning at church, we saw a stranger, a tall, well-dressed man with fair hair and bristling russet side whiskers that came down each side of his long, rather handsome face and ran into his mustache. After the service, he approached my father and introduced himself as Quincy Drummond, our new neighbor. His manner was polite and ingratiating, but I had a rather unpleasant impression of him, fancying that there was a touch of the theatrical about him— a kind of dash or affectation one might expect to find in an actor or a dandy—and it made me think that there was something false about him. He told my father that he had purchased extensive lands a little farther north. A timber business was to be his main concern, he said, hinting that he was also contemplating some interest in a saw mill. He had leased the place next to ours mainly as a residence in proximity to Charleston and his other property, and informed us that he was leaving the farming of it to some sharecropping freedmen.

On our way home in our old, rickety carriage, Papa expressed the opinion that Mr. Drummond was only here to make a fast dollar.

"I imagine that once he has made himself a neat little fortune, he will be on his way."

And good riddance to him then, I could almost hear my father adding in his thoughts.

When we reached the drive leading up to our house on our return each Sunday morning, we were always greeted by the sharp little barks of our dog as he trotted out to meet the carriage. This was Isham's pet, a fearless little black terrier of great energy and self-importance. His name was Wasp, and he quickly became fast friends with me and Matthew after we made Brewton Farm our home. Wasp seemed to sense Isham's infirmity, and was protective of him, but he unmistakably preferred our company. The dog was a pest sometimes, and liked to worry my chickens, but he was a source of amusement, and sometimes, a good watch dog. Once he ran off a man who was trying to steal one of our hogs. Wasp would sometimes go off on his own for hours or a day or two, but would always return to us. The family grew fond of him, and Mama would begin to fret when the little fellow was away for more than a night.

In December, when the weather turned cold enough, it was hog killing time. We had only a few hogs fat enough for slaughter, but Papa needed all of us to assist him in some way. Even Mama helped after the butchering was done, tending to the smaller pots for the cooking of the fat and souse meat. Though I had seen a little of this gory but necessary process in Summerton, I had never actually participated in it until we came to Brewton Farm. Being a city girl, I was accustomed to obtaining meat from the butcher's shop, but now that we no longer lived in town, we had to provide and preserve meat ourselves. I found it all very distasteful, and yet I was very thankful to have ham and sausage for at least part of the winter, and lard for cooking.

About a week before Christmas, on a fine, sunny weekday afternoon, Mr. Drummond drove up to our house in a fine new buggy pulled by a sleek, handsome black horse. Hearing Wasp's barking, Mama came out to the porch, and Mr. Drummond politely greeted her and asked her if he might speak with Mr. Campbell. I was nearby, and ran up to see the beautiful horse and pet it. Wasp kept barking, and I had to shoo him off.

"Careful, Mattie," Mama said to me, seeing that I was reaching out to stroke the horse's soft muzzle.

"Oh, he is very gentle, Mrs. Campbell," Mr. Drummond assured her. "There is no danger."

"My husband is working at the barn," Mama informed our guest. "Mattie can take you to him."

Mr. Drummond got down from his carriage, tied up his horse, and followed me to the barn. It was an unusually warm day in December, and Papa was wiping perspiration from his brow as he toiled under a cloudless sky. He had nearly finished replacing all the boards that had been missing from one side of the big barn, and was planing down a final piece. I called to him, and he looked surprised to turn and find me in the company of our new neighbor.

"Mr. Drummond has come to see you, Papa," I announced.

"I'll not take up too much of your time, Mr. Campbell," he said. "I see you are busy."

"What brings you here today, sir?" my father inquired, putting aside his tool and brushing sawdust from his shirt and sleeves.

"A business proposition," was Mr. Drummond's prompt answer.

Papa seemed taken aback by his reply. I was very curious about all this, but pretended that I wasn't. I stayed close by and started picking a few little yellow wildflowers that were still in bloom as if I were paying no attention to their conversation.

Mr. Drummond explained that he was of a mind to make Charleston his home, and thought he might wish to associate himself with a mercantile establishment, perhaps a cotton factor—something along those lines.

"I understand there is considerable difficulty in the transportation of cotton in the state," my father remarked doubtfully.

"Oh, that will improve in time," Mr. Drummond replied in a very confident tone. "Of that I am sure. And there is money to be made in it yet. The prices are high, you know."

Papa eyed him warily. The gentleman then came to his proposition.

"I understand you have much experience in the business, Mr. Campbell," he said. "And you doubtless have many connections in Charleston and the state. A newcomer to the business would find that experience and those connections quite valuable. What I am proposing to you, sir, having some capital at my disposal, is a business partnership."

Papa did not answer right away, except to repeat faintly, "A business partnership."

He seemed to be mulling over what Mr. Drummond had proposed, and as he did, his eyes wandered down to his own calloused hands, his worn out shoes, and threadbare trousers. I then saw him cut a glance at the handsome clothes of Mr. Drummond, who was wearing an expensive fawn-colored suit, an embroidered silk vest of green, and shiny new patent leather boots. He waited patiently for Papa's response, pulling out a fine white cotton handkerchief to wipe his brow, and as he did a ring of gold and onyx on his well-manicured hand flashed in the sun.

My father finally answered, saying, "I will consider your proposition, sir, if you will put it in writing, so that I may have some idea of the arrangements you have in mind."

Mr. Drummond smiled broadly.

"I will do that, Mr. Campbell," he said. "I will have something in writing for you soon. I'm sure we can work out an arrangement that will be agreeable to you."

They talked a little while longer, and afterward Mr. Drummond left and went back to his carriage. I thought Papa would go back to his work, but as I finished up my flower gathering, I was surprised to look up and see him standing perfectly still, lost in thought. His brow was contracted, as though he was contemplating something unpleasant rather than the reverse.

I approached him with my little bouquet of wildflowers and tilted my head curiously.

"Mattie," he said. "What did you hear of our conversation?"

"Oh...I heard a good bit," I answered sheepishly.

"Don't say anything about it to Matt or your

mother. Will you do that for me? Nothing may come of
it, you see."

"Yes, Papa," I muttered, and as I studied his face
again, I noticed that he looked ashamed.

* * *

A few days later, just two days before Christmas in
fact, a letter arrived for Papa. It was from Mr.
Drummond, and was accompanied by a document that
laid out the terms of a business partnership. Papa read
both papers very carefully that afternoon, and after
supper, I heard him talking the matter over with Mama.
I came into the parlor where they sat, and since I already
knew about Mr. Drummond's offer, Papa did not seem
to mind my eavesdropping.

Mama had received the news with some
consternation, and I was not surprised. Despite the hope
of renewed prosperity it brought, a business association
with one of our former enemies was an unpleasant, even
repugnant prospect to contemplate. As Papa talked to
her with a subdued, serious demeanor, I could tell that
deep inside, he was wrestling with uncertainty, and
worse, a sense of humiliation and shame. It was as
though he feared it was an act of disloyalty to his state.
He could see that Mama did not like this proposal of a
partnership with Mr. Drummond, and I knew that he
cringed inwardly at the thought of her disapproval. That
Mama might consider him capable of doing something

dishonorable—well, nothing in the world would have hurt Papa more than that.

When my father had explained all the terms of the agreement Mr. Drummond proposed, he paused and waited for her response. She looked very grave and thoughtful, but no answer came from her for a long while.

"What is your opinion, Margaret dear?" Papa pressed her, pained with suspense. "What do you think?"

After another silence she replied, "I think you ought to make it a matter of prayer, Joseph. Then whatever you decide will be for the best."

Papa looked a little relieved at this and said, "In his letter Mr. Drummond writes that he is in no hurry for an answer, that I may take my time to think over the matter, and so I shall, and make it a matter of prayer as you say."

Making a nod of assent, Mama rose solemnly and left the room. Papa went to a writing table and began a letter of reply to our neighbor, and after a few minutes he looked up at me and said, "Mr. Drummond asked in a postscript if he might be permitted to hunt in our woods occasionally. I am going to allow it, but I will ask him to give notice before he comes onto the property."

"I will tell Matthew," I replied.

"Yes, please do. I don't want Matt going out

hunting when there is another shooter in the woods."

My father soon finished his letter and sat back in his chair meditatively.

I ventured to ask, "Did you give Mr. Drummond an answer about the other matter?"

"I told him I would consider his offer, and give him an answer within a month's time," said Papa.

When Christmas arrived, there was no exchange of gifts, but everyone received a piece of clothing or two — plain and useful garments for work. There were no novelties, no trinkets or baubles, no candies, no luxuries or fineries. It was the most austere holiday my family had ever celebrated. Though our meal was somewhat more plentiful than usual, it was not fancy, and the only treat was a dessert of apple pie.

On Christmas Eve, after supper, my father built up a blazing fire in the parlor, and we all gathered around the hearth. For the evening's entertainment, I read aloud *A Christmas Carol*. Papa, digesting an unusually large meal, sometimes dozed off during the course of the story, but everyone else listened with due attention, their faces colored by the fire's bright orange glow. Even my fidgety brother was relatively still and attentive, and Isham, sitting open-mouthed and cross-legged on the floor, listened to the reading with all the concentration his poor wandering mind could muster, especially when the ghosts appeared — Marley in chains, and the spirits of

Christmas past, present and future.

That night in my bed, I dreamed of days gone by, and Christmas in Charleston before the war. I was in my favorite store, Kerrison's—a large, grand, beautiful establishment filled with all kinds of delightful, desirable goods. I walked down the long aisles bordered on both sides by handsome mahogany counters, and passing by one of the tall ornamental columns, I gazed up at the ornate carved ceilings and the beautiful cast iron chandeliers where gas lights burned in globes of milk glass. I moved through each department, selecting for myself or for a gift something from each one, filling my arms with toiletries, pairs of gloves, silk slippers, ribbons, and many other little luxuries. In my dream, it was also the Christmas season and, while I waited for my purchases to be wrapped, I warmed my hands at one of the handsome iron stoves that heated the store.

When I left Kerrison's and walked outside, a blast of frigid air made me shiver. I woke up shivering. It was a very cold night, and my quilt had slipped off the bed, leaving me only the covering of a thin sheet.

* * *

I saw the ghost for the first time just after the Christmas holiday.

It was on a Sunday evening at dusk, and I was at my hen-house making sure all my chickens were comfortable in their roosts and safe for the night. I was just about to bolt the door, when I heard my feathered friends begin to chatter with a low, fretful clucking. Something had disturbed them, but I knew they were safe, so I wondered if they were sensing something threatening outside their shelter.

It was getting quite dark as I looked around me. The edge of the woods was not far away, and suddenly, I heard a distinct rustle from that direction. Of course it may have been nothing more than a fox or a raccoon or some other little creature, but I was immediately filled with a strange apprehension. My head was still full of Marley and Dickens' Christmas ghosts, and for a few moments, despite my proud disbelief in such things, I felt at least a little afraid, and kept my eyes fixed on the spot from which the sound seemed to come.

And then I saw it—a figure of ghostly gray passing between the trees. It was there for a few seconds, and afterward abruptly disappeared. I felt a little faint, but I took a deep breath and backed away, and when I had moved back a few steps, I took off running and did not stop running until I reached the kitchen house.

I went inside to find Bess right away.

"I saw it!" I told her, panting more with excitement and drama than physical exertion. "I saw the ghost!"

"Was he gray?" she inquired, wide-eyed. The old cook's eyes were large and somewhat bulging, and the whites of them were not white but a brownish yellow, like old ivory, or white cloth that had been dyed with tea.

"He was," I replied.

"That's the soldier's ghost," she said, with a knowing nod.

"I didn't believe in ghosts before, but now I think I might," I confessed. "I really think so, Bess. I'm sure I did not imagine what I saw."

"Mm, huh," she uttered in her drawn out, singsong way, still nodding.

"Why is he haunting this place?" I wondered aloud.

"Mebbe he died 'round here," Bess speculated.

"But there wasn't any fighting around here," said I, puzzled.

She reminded me that the Confederate soldiers out of Charleston had marched through the area. She had seen them with her own eyes as they passed by, evacuating the area in the winter of 1865, when it was feared that General Sherman's large army was threatening an attack on the city, the Confederate forces in the area being much smaller in number.

Maybe, old Bess went on, contemplating a likely scenario, maybe one of those soldiers was ill, and collapsed and died on the march, and was hastily buried somewhere on the farm.

She added, looking ominous, it might be that

"them Yankees" had seen a new grave when they came through a little later on, and had dug it up, thinking that they might find valuables buried in the spot rather than a corpse. They may have desecrated his body, so that his troubled spirit lingered in this place, seeking some kind of amends, or vengeance.

"Oh, that is terrible!" I exclaimed.

I dismissed the idea at first, but then, the more I thought about it, the more likely it seemed to me to be a reasonable explanation for the spirit's presence. We had heard stories of Yankee soldiers digging up graves and breaking into tombs and burial vaults looking for valuables during the war, and we knew them to be true. Our own family cemetery at Brewton Farm had suffered such depredations. When we first came to live there, we found that several of our ancestors' graves had been excavated and vandalized, and that some of the stone markers had been toppled or smashed to pieces. All this desecration had angered Papa a great deal, though he was glad to find that the oldest of our family graves, a marble tomb that rested above the ground, had remained untouched.

After my conversation with Bess I went to tell my mother and father about the great event. They were seated in the dining room, and I came in and very solemnly and importantly announced that I had seen the ghost.

My parents were nonchalant.

"We do not believe in ghosts, dear," Mama said to me serenely.

Her reasoning was that they were not in the Bible, and therefore they did not exist. Papa seemed to be in agreement with her on the matter.

"But I saw it with my own eyes!" I protested.

"You have quite an imagination, Mattie," my father countered. "Remember how you once told us you saw fairies in flowers?"

"I was very young when I told you that! I was just a baby then!" I defended myself.

I tried to convince them that I had not been imagining things, that I had actually seen something in the woods, but I had no success. Frustrated by their indifference and disbelief, I went to find Matthew. I found him with Isham. They were sitting by the parlor fire whittling pieces of wood, making slingshots. As I told him about seeing the ghost, he pressed me for every detail, but continued with his whittling. Isham's mouth dropped open a little at the mention of the ghost, and he grew very still.

"Was he floating above the ground?" asked Matthew. "Did you see his face? What did he sound like?"

"He didn't make any sound," I replied, "except a rustling in the leaves, I think. I couldn't tell if he was floating, but it seemed to me that he moved just like a ghost, and then disappeared. I couldn't see his face."

"You know, Mattie," said my brother, "I found an old book of clippings in the bureau in my room, and some of them were newspaper stories about some terrible murders that went on near here. Maybe that ghost is one of the murderers they hanged, or one of the men they killed!"

"Where is that book?" I asked eagerly. "I want to see those stories."

Matthew jumped up and went to his room, returning very quickly with an old album in his hands.

"I think Uncle Pink kept this book," he said, plopping down on the floor with it. "Now let me see..."

He thumbed through a number of pages, and when he found what he was looking for, he handed me the book.

"It's from an old Charleston newspaper. See the date of 1819?"

Pasted into the album, I found several columns of a newspaper with that date, and other columns and writings dated 1820, all of which reported the story of the notorious criminals John and Lavinia Fisher. As I read the first one aloud, Isham put aside his slingshot and listened intently.

"A gang of desperadoes have for some time past occupied certain houses, and infested the road leading to this city, in the vicinity of Ashley Ferry, practicing every deception upon the unwary, and frequently committing robberies upon defenseless travelers. As they could not be identified, and thereby brought to punishment, it was determined by a number of citizens, to break them up, and they accordingly proceeded to a house commonly called the Five-Mile House, where they found a number assembled, who were ordered to quit the building within fifteen minutes' time; but not showing a disposition to do so quietly, the house was set afire and burnt to the ground. To such an extent had these outlaws carried their excesses of late, that wagoners and others coming into town were under the necessity of carrying their rifles in their hands for defense against robbery; and when the outlaws could lure the unwary traveler into their house, he was sure to be either swindled out of his money by gambling, or robbed of it in any moment of unguarded security."

"Read the next one," Matthew urged me, continuing with his whittling. "It's an excellent piece."

I read on.

"In Saturday's Courier we gave particulars of a set of outlaws, occupants of a small house five miles outside town, who had been driven out and the building burnt to the ground. The outlaws then resorted to a house one mile above, and beat the person in possession of it in a most inhuman manner before he escaped into the woods and made his way back to town. The next morning, the gang stopped a traveler upon the road, beat him cruelly, and robbed him. The Sheriff of this District collected a posse of citizens and proceeded on Saturday to the spot, surrounded the house, and seized its occupants (three men and two women). The posse found in an outhouse the hide of a cow, which had been recently killed, and identified to be the property of one of our citizens. We trust these decisive steps will restore quiet to the neighborhood, and enable our country brethren to enter and leave the city without fear of insult or robbery."

I perused the next article, which revealed the names of two of the criminals—John Fisher and his wife Lavinia—and reported that the bones of men had been found in the cellar of the outlaws' house.

"Oh, they were not only robbers, but murderers, too!" I gasped.

"Oh, yes!" said Matthew. "I told you that, didn't I? And they were hanged!"

My eyes wandered to some clippings which appeared to be pages taken from a small book, and over which was inscribed in in Uncle Pink's handsome penmanship, "A visit to the gallows." As I read this account, I could not help but be moved by the writer's description of the doomed husband and wife sentenced to death, guilty criminals though they were, as they left the jail and traveled to the gallows.

"The prisoners had provided themselves, at their private expense, with loose white garments, which they put on over their clothes. They threw themselves once more into each other's arms, and bade each other an eternal farewell. The unhappy victims descended the stairs, arm in arm, to a coach waiting at the prison door, and the procession slowly moved forward. Arriving within sight of the gibbet, which was erected a little way out of the city, we remember the horrible picture of despair exhibited in the countenance of Fisher, when he first beheld the frightful reality. His cheek assumed a livid paleness; his eyes involuntarily closed; a tremor shook his frame; he almost sunk into the arms of the master-spirit that now presided over his destiny. He made, at this moment, a prodigious effort to recover himself. He drew his wife, with a convulsive grasp, to his bosom, and in a few seconds, looked up, nerved for the issue. The coach now reached the spot. Fisher mounted the scaffold, and cast his eyes mournfully around upon the large gathering of spectators. Not so his wife. She positively refused to go up. Neither remonstrances, nor persuasions, nor threats, could avail. The constables were at length constrained to resort to bodily force, and she was almost dragged to the stand. This unhappy woman could not believe it possible that she was then destined to die. She called upon the multitude to rescue her, and stretched forth her trembling arms, imploring pity. She stamped and raved, with incoherent wildness, and silence hung over the vast assembly, broken only by the shrieks (truly demoniacal) of this very maniac upon the verge of eternity! Nothing could be more appalling. She was totally unprepared to die. It was pitiable; it was truly heart-rending to behold this unhappy husband, himself just about to perish and, needing every moment for his own soul's sake, bending, with interest the most intense, towards his frantic wife and, in the tenderest accents, urging her to make her peace with heaven."

"Oh, that is so very sad," I observed, almost in tears.

"Read the one about their hanging!" Matthew urged me on gleefully.

I found a newspaper article dated February 19, 1820, which stated as follows, "THE EXECUTION of John and Lavinia Fisher, for highway robbery, took place yesterday, in the suburbs of the city, agreeably to their sentence. They were taken from the jail about a quarter before one o'clock, in a carriage, in which, besides the prisoners, was Rev. Dr. Furman, and an officer of the police. They were guarded by the Sheriff of the District, with his assistants, and a small detachment of cavalry. Arrived at the fatal spot, some time was spent in conversation and prayer. Fisher protested his innocence of the crime for which he was about to die to the last, but admitted that he had lived a wicked and abandoned life. He met his fate with great firmness, and expressed his obligations to the new Sheriff for his kindness and humanity. His wife did not display so much of fortitude or resignation. She appeared to be impressed with a belief, to the last moment, that she would be pardoned. A little past two o'clock the husband and wife embraced each other upon the platform, for the last time in this world, when the fatal signal was given. The drop fell, and they were launched into eternity. She died without a struggle or a groan; but it was some minutes before he expired and ceased to struggle. After hanging the usual time, their bodies were taken down and conveyed to Potter's Field, where they were interred. The crowd that attended the execution was immense. May the awful example strike deep into their hearts, and may it have the effect intended, by deterring others from pursuing those vicious paths which end in infamy and death."

I felt my heart pounding with horror as I finished reading. Isham was actually trembling, and swallowing hard, but Matthew repeated loudly with dramatic relish, "Infamy and death!" He then looked up at our appalled expressions and laughed.

"You're such a goose, Mattie!" he snickered. "Isham, too! You ought not to read such stories."

"But you asked me to read them!" I fumed.

He laughed again, and shook his head.

"Well, perhaps I ought not to have read them to Isham," I said with a huff. "But you suggested that one of the Fishers, or one of their victims, might be our ghost!"

"It is possible, isn't it?" Matthew replied. "That house they lived in wasn't too far from here. They died dressed in white, and white can look gray in the dark! Anyway, it's a good story."

"I suppose it is possible, but we never heard of any ghosts around here before the war. Old Bess insists that our ghost is a soldier."

"Was he wearing a uniform?"

"I don't know. He seemed to be dressed in a pale, grayish color, but you know that it's hard to see colors in the darkness."

"Bess thinks it a soldier's ghost, because he is dressed in gray, but maybe he isn't a soldier," my brother mused. He paused and fell deep in thought, and after a little while, he suddenly grew wide-eyed and comically slapped himself on the forehead.

"I know who the ghost is!" he cried. "Why didn't I think of it before?"

"Who is he, Matt?"

"It's one of our relatives whose grave was dug up! Remember when we came back to the farm for the first time, and found that the cemetery had been vandalized? It's one of those poor souls whose grave was desecrated by the soldiers! His rest has been disturbed, and he is haunting this place."

"But you and Papa reburied all the caskets, and filled the graves, and put the stones back," I reminded him. "Wouldn't that satisfy the haunting spirit?"

"How should I know? But evidently it has not satisfied him. He is a restless spirit."

* * *

One Sunday evening, as the family sat out on the porch and enjoyed some fine weather, we saw our cousin Isham walking past with some rope looped around one of his shoulders. Matthew and I watched him for a while, and when we saw that he was heading in the direction of the woods, both of us jumped up at the same time and scurried down the steps to catch up with him.

He stopped, and we asked him what he was doing.

"I'm going to catch that ghost," Isham announced, with a strange look of wonder and determination.

Matthew and I bit our lips to suppress smiles and the irrepressible laughter that was bubbling up in us.

"Well, good night to you," said my brother. Taking my hand, he led me off, and soon we both broke into a run to get to the house before we burst. We ran inside, and hearing our laughter and giggles, Mama left her chair on the porch and came into the parlor to find out what was so amusing.

"Isham has made up his mind to catch the ghost," I told her.

"Oh, dear," she murmured, casting her eyes upward with a little shake of the head. "Well, I suppose there is no harm in that."

"Unless he catches the ghost and brings him home!" Matthew howled, convulsed with laughter again.

"Yes, that might be awkward," Mama replied with a smile.

At supper the following evening, exercising great self-control, Matthew asked Isham how he was going to catch the ghost.

"What's this about a ghost?" said Papa, before our cousin could answer.

"The one I saw," I quickly replied.

"Old Bess has seen it, too," my brother added promptly.

"Oh, yes," Papa sighed, shaking his head. "I remember that nonsense now."

"It isn't nonsense," argued Matthew. "Others saw it, too. Old Bess told us so."

"Perhaps she's mistaken," Mama suggested tactfully.

I reminded her a second time that I myself had been a witness to this mysterious phantom. My mother and father exchanged a look of amused resignation, and said no more on the subject, but Matthew took up his questioning of Isham again.

"How do you propose to capture this ghost?" he inquired.

"I'm going to lie in wait for it," our cousin answered.

"And then what?"

"And then I will spring upon him, and catch hold of him, and have a rope ready to tie him up."

Fighting an impulse to laugh, Matthew clenched his teeth and cleared his throat so loudly that Mama scolded him.

"Isham," said my brother, after a deliberate pause, "a ghost is immaterial."

Our cousin did not seem to understand the meaning of the word.

"A ghost is like a cloud, or a puff of smoke," Matthew explained. "How could you tie up a puff of smoke, or even catch hold of it? Do you know what a ghost is?"

"Something that has come out of the grave," Isham replied.

"A ghost is a spirit—like an angel. You know what an angel is, don't you?"

Isham pondered this for a few moments, and then remarked, "Jacob wrestled with an angel, so he got hold of a spirit. That's in the Bible."

Looking genuinely surprised, my brother sighed, "Well, you have me there."

Chuckling and patting Isham on the shoulder, Papa said, "He does have you there, Matt. Isham, you made a very good point, my boy."

* * *

Though somewhat removed from the city, we had a few regular visitors to the farm, usually close relatives who called on Sundays. Another frequent caller was a former neighbor, Augustus Thomson, the youngest son of our pastor. Gus, as we all called him, had lived just next door to our house on Elizabeth Street in Charleston, and he and I were friends, and companions sometimes, though he was somewhat older.

He was a bright, energetic young man of twenty-one who was studying to become a lawyer. He worked in the office of one of Charleston's oldest and most prominent attorneys, although there was little in the way of any lucrative legal business going on in the city for many months after the war. The legal profession was in a shambles like everything else in the city, which was under military occupation, and in part, military rule, for a long while.

During the war, Gus and I were regular correspondents. Our friendship deepened through our many letters, and I think toward the end, he confided in me more than anyone else. When we moved to

Summerton he kept me abreast of all that was going on in dear old Charleston, and occasionally he would also write to my father and mother. The whole family liked him very much, and esteemed him as a fine person and a hero of the war.

Gus certainly did not consider himself a hero. He spent much of the war in Charleston, mostly serving in the Signal Corps, transmitting messages and reports from his posts of observation, one of which was the high windowed steeple of St. Michael's Church downtown. He was only seventeen when the war began, but as soon as his parents permitted it he enlisted in the army, and in the summer of 1862, he got his first taste of real fighting at the Battle of Secessionville on James Island. Even after witnessing the carnage of this terrible bloodbath, he was anxious to get into the thick of the fighting in Virginia, where his brothers, cousins, and friends were serving, and where he felt he ought to be. Year after year, Gus made applications for transfer, but nothing ever came of them, leaving him terribly disappointed and irked. He felt himself wasted in the Signal Corps, and capable of better things, and I suspect he was also eager to distinguish himself in military service, partly because such distinction would serve him in his pursuits later in life. He was an admittedly ambitious young man, full of self-confidence, and yet he was not selfish or immodest; he simply knew his own abilities and intellect, and was thankful for them, and confident that they were meant to take him far in life.

I had not seen much of Gus during the war, though he did come to visit us in Summerton once, on my sixteenth birthday. On his first visit to Brewton Farm, I was surprised to see that he had grown taller, and was sporting a carefully groomed and curled mustache. Not only had his looks changed, his experiences as a soldier had also changed and matured him in character, of course, and yet much of the boy remained in him, and he was full of fun and harmless nonsense, especially around me and Matthew, the companions of his childhood. With my father, Gus was usually more serious, and would often talk of his plans for his future. Now that he had chosen the law as his profession, he told Papa that he wanted to excel in it, and become a public man someday, and perhaps even go to Congress.

After Gus called on us a few times at the farm, I began to notice a change in him. He was still witty and whimsical, and a great talker, but at times he would fall into a kind of brief reverie or preoccupation while with us, and would then brighten and grow talkative and attentive again. It seemed to me that something was on his mind he would not reveal, and gradually, I noticed that these spells grew longer and more brooding. Knowing that Gus had a predominantly cheerful and optimistic nature, I wondered what exactly was troubling him. Heaven knows, there was much to trouble everyone in those days.

On a rainy Sunday afternoon after one of his visits, I was with Mama in the parlor, and she said to me, "You know, Mattie, one of these days, Gus is just going to burst out and ask you to marry him."

I was so surprised, I almost laughed.

"Ask me to marry him!" I cried incredulously.

"Mattie, why do you think he comes here on Sundays?" asked Mama. "You are seventeen now. Don't you see that he is interested in you, dear?"

"Well, he does look at me strangely sometimes," I mused. "But much of the time he just seems to be brooding."

"He is brooding about you," said my mother.

"I don't think so," I replied, though in fact I was beginning to wonder if she might be right.

I went off by myself to think over the matter. I was still in such a state of shock that I found it difficult to think clearly at first, but as I got used to the idea of Gus being a suitor, I was better able to properly assess the situation, or so I thought.

I walked into the library and sat down in the window seat. Gazing out at the rain, I contemplated my friend in this new light. He was a nice boy, and a good Christian, I reflected. He was very intelligent and well read, and meant to make something of himself someday.

He was not bad-looking, either, with a face and a physique that promised to improve with age. Yet, with all these good qualities, I did not feel what I thought I ought to feel for him as a prospective husband, and it was because I was comparing him to dear Micah — handsome, gallant, chivalrous Micah. Poor Gus! He paled in comparison to my shining knight, my ideal man, and seemed a rather meager fellow indeed.

Something else was also working against Gus. If he loves me, I asked myself, why doesn't he show it? Why doesn't he say affectionate or romantic things to me, or compose a love letter or a poem for me? Why, he had not so much as brought me a wildflower. As I pondered about Gus, I became convinced that there was not a romantic bone in his body.

If he does love me, he has a very peculiar way of showing it, I decided. It also seemed to me that his affections could not be of a very strong or passionate sort, and worse, it appeared that he was loath to admit them! His was a grudging, undemonstrative kind of affection, I thought. Apparently I did not inspire the sort of raptures that Marius felt for Cosette, and this wounded my girlish pride and vanity. I felt piqued and insulted, and quite indifferent about the whole matter. I simmered with these feelings for the rest of the week, and when Sunday came, and brought our usual caller, I did not smile at him once. I glowered instead, trying to match his frequent brooding expression, though Gus didn't seem to understand my meaning.

That afternoon Papa felt unwell and was taking a nap, and Matthew had gone to visit a friend. As Gus and I sat in the parlor with Mama, she kept studying us both in an odd way, and after about a quarter hour of conversation, she excused herself, saying that she had to go out for a few moments to attend to something in the kitchen. Her departure left Gus and me alone in the room. All of a sudden he looked up at me very seriously and intently.

"Why are you staring at me?" I asked in a peevish tone. "Glaring, I should say."

"I don't mean to glare," he replied, though his expression did not change.

"Well you are glaring," said I.

He asked me if I was feeling unwell.

"I feel just fine," was the answer I gave in a haughty, staccato manner.

"I'm glad, Miss Mattie," he said. "I'm very glad because I have come here today to tell you something."

"Tell me, then," I sniffed. "What is it you have to say to me?"

"Well," he muttered, looking uncomfortable. "Well, the truth is…what I have to say is, I love you."

My mouth almost dropped open—not at what he said, but at the way he said it.

"You look unpleasantly surprised," Gus observed uneasily.

"Well, you almost sound angry about what you said to me!" I replied, to his great surprise.

"I am not angry!"

"Well if not angry, then resentful. Yes, you sound resentful when you say that to me."

"I am not angry, nor resentful, Miss Mattie," he said, gasping a little. "I don't know how you have such an idea. It's just that…honestly…it is very hard for me to say such things to you. I – I've been trying to work up the courage to express my feelings to you."

"You are not romantic in the least," I complained, lifting my chin and turning my face away from him.

Gus sighed and lowered his head, but almost immediately, he jumped to his feet and said, "Miss Mattie, I have made my feelings known to you. If, in time, you think you might ever return them, please inform me."

And then he was gone. I kept my seat, fuming, and my brother, who had just returned home, wandered into the parlor and asked what the matter was.

"Why did Gus run out of the house? And why did his face look like a storm cloud?"

I hesitated to tell Matthew what had happened between us, but he managed to wheedle it out of me, and when I finished speaking, my brother eyed me scornfully.

"So Gus is not romantic enough for you," he jeered. "What did you want him to say? Tell you how beautiful you are? Well, you are not beautiful. You are a plain girl, Mattie. Yes, you are smart and bookish, and so is he, and that is probably why he loves you, but would you have him lie to you—pay you silly compliments that are not true? Hah! You ought to be glad and grateful that such a fine boy loves you!"

I was fuming even more now, and wanted to strangle my brother, but all at once, I burst into tears and ran out of the room, having just realized that everything he said was true. I hurried to my room and had a good cry.

Later, I found a mirror and took a good look at myself, with Matthew's words still ringing in my ears. My face was long like my mother's, but not as narrow and delicate. It was broader like my father's face, and when I wasn't smiling, my lips were downturned and naturally frowning. My nose was unremarkable, and I had always wished that my eyes were brighter, and blue rather than brown. I did not often examine myself in the mirror this way, but after gazing at my reflection for a while, I had to admit that I had not grown into a beauty. I was plain, as my brother said.

"But not so plain," I thought, still gazing at myself, "that Gus could not love me. He does love me."

And the more I thought about it, the more I became certain that, despite his faults, I could love him, too, and that I had always loved him as a friend. Now he wished to be my lover and husband, and friendship seemed at least a place to start for me.

"I will allow him to court me," I said to myself. "And we'll see what happens."

Then and there I sat down and wrote him a letter, and told him honestly how I felt, and how we might proceed. The following Sunday, Gus paid another visit to our house after church. His face no longer looked like a storm cloud, as Matthew had put it. On the contrary, he seemed very happy and high-spirited. We sat together on the porch, and with great enthusiasm, he told me about all the things he was learning about the law from Mr. McCrady, the great attorney, going on and on for nearly a quarter hour.

"He says I am very quick to learn," Gus informed me proudly. "And that I will certainly make a fine lawyer someday. Someday! That sounds a little too far off for my taste. I shall be his partner, or someone else's, in a year's time, you mark my word. Of course there isn't much work now, but things will get back to normal in due time."

Gus paused, and was about to go on along the same lines, I could tell, but he stopped himself and instead turned all his attention to me.

"What are you reading these days, Miss Mattie?" he asked. "Tell me about it."

I embarked on a lengthy answer, and as I talked, Gus began to look at me in a way he had never done before. His was a tender, wistful look, and I must say it affected me. At one point in our conversation, quite unexpectedly (for both of us, I imagine), he took my hand and kissed it. From that time forward, his manner toward me changed for the better, and my feelings for him began to undergo a transformation into something much deeper than friendship.

* * *

One Thursday morning we noticed that Wasp had gone off on one of his mysterious expeditions. The next day, Papa found that one of our pigs had been stolen, and he vowed that he would get himself a better watch dog, for Wasp had become too unreliable.

I had finished all my chores early that day, and thought I might begin reading a new book, but I kept thinking about Wasp, and worrying about him, and an idea formed in my mind that I ought to go out and look for him. Matthew, Isham and Papa were out repairing some fences, and Mama and old Bess were busy cooking and preserving various foodstuffs. I walked out to the kitchen house and asked Mama if I might go out and hunt for Wasp. I knew that she was worried about the dog, too.

We had harvested some apples from the orchard, and in the midst of her other food preparations, my mother was also making some apple butter and had assigned Bess the task of stirring the pot while it cooked over the fire. As I came in calling for her, Mama was checking the progress of the sauce and gestured to me to wait until she was finished. I saw a book open on a table, *The Ladies' Receipt Book,* and while I waited I perused the receipt, or recipe, for apple butter.

"To make this article according to German custom," it said, "let a bushel of apples be pared, quartered, and the cores removed. Meanwhile let a barrel of clear new cider be boiled down to one half, and when this is done commit the prepared apples to the cider, and henceforth let the boiling go on briskly and systematically. To accomplish the main design, the contents must be stirred without cessation, that they do not become attached to the side of the kettle, and be burned. Let this stirring go on till the liquid thickens and the amalgamated cider and apples become as thick as hasty pudding. Then throw in seasoning of pulverized allspice, when it may be considered as finished and committed to future pots for use. This is apple butter, and will keep sweet for many years."

"Mmm, something sweet," I murmured dreamily. I had always loved confections and sweets of any kind, and could hardly wait to taste this delicious butter on a biscuit or toast. We seldom enjoyed such treats.

When my mother was finished she asked me what I wanted, and I made my request. She hesitated, but gave me permission to go as long as I did not roam too far from the house.

"And no more than an hour, Mattie," she added firmly, getting back to her other work. "See that you come home within an hour's time."

I promised that I would, and skipped back to the house to fetch my shawl and hat. Pausing on the porch, I gazed off in the direction that I had last seen Wasp. I remembered catching a glimpse of him chasing a rabbit into the woods in one particular place, and I knew that he had gone into the thickest, most overgrown part of the woods that stretched as far as the road to Charleston. I would look there, I decided, and having explored in this area with Matthew on one or two occasions just after our arrival at Brewton Farm, I determined not to let the new dress I had received for Christmas get torn or snagged in the briars and brambles. I went into my brother's room, found a few of his old clothes, and dressed myself like a boy. When I had pinned my hair up and donned one of his hats, I was ready for the hunt.

This was all great fun, I thought, as I anticipated a nice little adventure all on my own, and perhaps a triumphant return with Wasp. I must confess, now that I had seen the ghost, I also prided myself on being rather brave and daring, though perhaps going out alone in broad daylight was really not so bold of me.

From the house, I ran to the woods, suspecting that if Papa saw me he would not allow this little excursion. Once there, I sought out a narrow deer path that Matthew and I had used before. I picked my way along, pushing away overhanging branches, and trying to avoid the briars and undergrowth along the route, but it was not quite the challenge I had expected. It seemed to me that someone had been using the path lately, though I was not sure of this, wondering whether it was only that many of the plants growing along the path had dwindled and died back for the winter. I moved on, and every now and then called out for Wasp.

It had been a sunny day, but the clouds began to gather in mid-afternoon, making the woods a little darker and gloomier. Eventually I came to a familiar sight—the overturned trunk of a massive, ancient tree— and just after passing it I scrambled over a tangle of broken limbs that had fallen across the path. By this time, I estimated that I had been making my way through the woods for a half hour, and I knew that it was time to turn back, as I had promised Mama, but I couldn't resist going on just a little farther, having noticed that there was a kind of clearing just ahead. As I continued I could see the stumps of some small pine trees that looked as though they had been recently cut, and when I stepped into the little clearing, a surprising sight met my eyes.

Someone had constructed an enclosure, a pen, and trapped inside it were several pigs. I recognized one of them—she belonged to us! The animals grunted and squealed a little as I approached, and as I drew closer I noticed that much of the pen was made of white wooden boards. So that is where the boards of our barn went to, I thought, and the person who had taken them was also the culprit who had stolen our pig. Obviously he had stolen from other farmers, too.

I knelt down at the gate of the pen and made a move to open it and let the pigs out, but quickly thought better of it. I decided that I ought to fetch Papa instead. He would know what to do. When the animals saw me at the gate, they set up more of a racket, thinking that they were getting fed or released, I suppose, and I did not hear the sound of approaching footsteps at first. By the time I got to my feet and looked around, a man was entering the clearing from the opposite direction.

He was a dirty, coarse-looking fellow I had never seen before. He was holding a canvas sack, and I don't know whether it contained anything, or if he meant to carry off something in it, but when he saw me he immediately dropped it to the ground and glared at me savagely.

"What's this? A thief!" he had the gall to say.

I was momentarily frozen with fear and indignation, but I quickly turned and began to run back the way I had come, and the stranger took off after me in a flash. I ran as fast as I could, but he was faster, and was soon just behind me on the path.

"Come here, boy!" he cried angrily. "I'll git ye anyhow!"

My heart was pounding with terror as I fled, and I had never been so afraid in my life. He will catch me, I was thinking, and I cried out desperately to God for help. I kept running, and as I neared the great fallen tree that overshadowed the path, foolishly looking at it rather than my feet, I suddenly came against the branches in the path. They caused me to trip, and I fell. I immediately jumped up, but it was too late. The man was upon me, and seized me by the sleeve.

"Let me go!" I shrieked. I was so overwhelmed with fear that a wave of dizziness swept over me.

He secured a tight grip on my arm and started dragging me back toward the clearing.

"You come with me," he grumbled. "You ain't goin' nowhere."

I struggled to break loose from his hold, but he was very strong, and very determined. Growing more hysterical, I began to scream for help. He tried to cover my mouth with one of his filthy hands, but I shook my head wildly and managed to cry out several times.

Finally, he pressed his hand over my mouth securely, and though I continued to struggle and resist, his strength was too much for me. I began to feel faint again, but I was suddenly roused by a loud noise nearby. Someone had fired a gun! The thief stopped, looked around frantically, and then let go of me and ran away. I staggered and nearly fell, but caught myself, putting my hand to a tree trunk, and the next moment, I heard a familiar voice.

"Is that the Campbell boy?" someone called out, and soon a man holding a rifle appeared in the path. It was Mr. Drummond.

"What's the matter, son?" he asked, but he was soon close enough to see that I was not Matthew.

"I heard someone crying out, and fired a shot into the air," he said. "Was that you?"

Catching my breath, I nodded and told him about the thief.

"What are you doing out in these woods?" he asked me.

"I was looking for our dog Wasp," I replied. "He has been gone for three days now."

"Didn't your father tell you that I would be hunting on his property today?"

"No, sir, he didn't. He didn't know that I was going out."

Mr. Drummond looked very concerned and very

relieved at the same time.

"Well," he said, "I am glad that I was here to help you, Miss Campbell, though it is very disconcerting to think that you were out here while I was hunting."

I thanked him for helping me, and he offered to escort me back to the house. Believe me, I was very glad for his company. When we reached the edge of the woods, I saw Papa and Matthew leaving the house showing signs of great agitation. They had just learned of my absence, and were coming out to look for me. Of course they had also heard the gunshot.

My mother, who had followed them out as far as the porch steps, saw me first in the distance, knowing that it was me despite the way I was dressed, and she called out my name. Papa and Matthew saw me an instant later, and took off at a run to meet me. Father and son looked utterly dumbfounded to find me in Matthew's clothes, and in the company of Mr. Drummond.

"Mattie!" Papa exclaimed. "Where have you been? Are you all right?"

"I was out looking for Wasp, Papa," I answered. "The man who stole our pig was in the woods, and Mr. Drummond chased him off and—"

"Let me go after him, Papa!" Matthew interrupted excitedly.

"You'll do no such thing, young man!" my father

snapped back at him.

"I ran away from the man," I went on, "but he caught me—"

The look of shock and horror on Papa's face stopped my speech, and as I faltered, Mr. Drummond spoke up calmly.

"I don't think any harm came to your daughter," he said. "I fired a warning shot, and the man let her go and disappeared into the woods. I imagine he only meant to restrain her to give himself time to get away with his stealings."

"He thought I was a boy, Papa," I added.

My father was breathing heavily, but with each breath, he grew more composed, and, finally, letting out a sigh, he turned to Mr. Drummond and held out his right hand.

"I am inexpressibly grateful to you, sir," he said to our neighbor. "It was God's providence that put you in these woods today to protect our Mattie."

"I am happy to be of service to you, Mr. Campbell," my protector replied, shaking Papa's hand vigorously.

That night, Papa gave me a stern scolding about going off without his knowledge or permission, but he and Mama were so relieved that no harm had come to me that they sent me to bed with many hugs and kisses afterward. I fetched a book to read, and as I was about to go upstairs to my room, I saw them sitting in the parlor engaged in hushed, earnest conversation, while my father was holding a piece of paper in his hands. I guessed that it was Mr. Drummond's business proposal.

* * *

As the new year of 1866 began, the winter turned bitterly cold. Matthew spent much of his time chopping firewood, and Isham was assigned the responsibility of gathering sticks for kindling. Papa had instructed our cousin to always be home by suppertime, and not to go out again after dark, but Matthew and I knew that Isham had gone out at night at least once since our father forbade it. Our cousin had become quite obsessed with finding and catching the ghost.

"Where is Isham?" Mama asked us one evening.

No one had seen him since supper. My brother offered up a suggestion.

"He must be out ghost hunting again."

"In this weather!" Mama exclaimed. "The only thing he will catch tonight is his death of cold!"

Papa told Matthew to put on a coat and go and look for Isham, and bring him home immediately.

"May I go out, too?" I asked him. "I wish to make sure the hen-house is secure. There is some wind tonight, and I'm afraid the door might be blown open."

Papa consented, but told me to come back to the house as soon as I had finished my task. Matthew and I bundled up in our warmest coverings and went out together in to the cold, breezy air. We did not carry lanterns. The frigid black sky was perfectly clear, and a full moon gave us plenty of light to see by. Matthew walked me to the hen-house, meaning to wait until I was finished and then watch me until I was safely back at the house. I found that I had bolted the door properly, and that it was in no danger of flying open from the light winds swirling about us, despite the occasional strong gust.

The occupants of the hen-house were clucking and making little prolonged, fretful growls, but I thought it was our unexpected presence here after dark that had perturbed them. Matthew speculated that there might be a fox or a wild dog about.

"Did you see something?" I asked him.

When I received no answer, I turned and discovered that he was standing very still, as if frozen, and staring off in the direction of the family cemetery.

"What is it?" I whispered. "Is it Isham?"

"Hush, Mattie!" he quickly returned, also whispering.

I came to his side and looked in the same direction he was staring, and then I saw what he saw—a dim light, low to the ground. A faint metallic sound came to our ears, and the light disappeared.

"Someone is among the graves," he said. "That was

a dark lantern, I'm sure of it. That sound was someone closing it."

"Isham?" I wondered.

"Where would he get one of those? We don't have one," replied my brother.

"Oh, he is always turning up with strange things he has found," I reminded him.

"Yes, that's true. Let's go and see what he's up to," Matthew suggested, now with a hint of mischief in his voice.

Forgetting, or rather ignoring Papa's instructions that I should return to the house promptly, I followed my brother into the trees, and for a while we stealthily picked our way along a deer path that skirted the edge of the woods. The bare boughs of the trees rustled in the cold breezes, and though I kept close to Matthew, I felt a little afraid in the darkness. I almost cried out when some wild bird we disturbed rushed upward out of the underbrush, flapping its wings wildly in alarm. I made no sound, but I was so startled that I stopped, and Matthew seized my hand and pulled it to get me going again.

When we were near the cemetery, we left the path and slowly and, as quietly as possible, made our way to the edge of the woods and came out behind the great oak tree, its trunk as wide as three men. Crouching down on our knees, we crawled around it and peered through a tangle of dead brush—and what we saw made our mouths drop open.

The tall figure of a man was leaning over the raised tomb of our great, great grandfather. We could see that he was holding and working with some kind of rod or pole, and though his back was to us, we could distinguish who it was—our neighbor Mr. Drummond. No one else we knew wore such fine clothes. To our shock and horror, we soon realized that he was attempting to pry out a slab of stone from one end of the tomb. Some of the vines of ivy that had encased much of the marble sides had been ripped away, and lay strewn across the ground at his feet.

Matthew turned to me grimly and made a motion indicating that we should go back the way we came. I knew he meant for us to go back to the house and fetch Papa. We were just starting to back out on our hands and knees, when suddenly, a loud cry pierced the air. The sound seemed to come from above us, and we looked up and saw and heard a movement in the largest branch of the oak tree, the one that reached out farthest over the graves.

A moment later, something swiftly dropped down from that branch, and we instantly recognized the form to be that of our cousin Isham. He fell directly on the back of Mr. Drummond, who was momentarily flattened against the tomb, but quickly raised up and freed himself from his attacker's weak grasp around his neck. Being the larger and stronger man, he easily subdued Isham and held him down over the stone, beating his head against it. Our cousin went limp, and we saw a length of rope fall from his hand to the ground.

All this happened very quickly as Matthew and I watched, petrified with fear and astonishment, but when Isham began to cry out in pain, Matthew made a movement to get to his feet. Terrified for his safety, I automatically seized his legs and would not let go.

"Mattie, no!" he gasped, tripping and falling to the ground again.

The next moment, we both looked up when we heard another startling cry, a warlike yell, and simultaneous with it, we saw an object fly past us and strike Mr. Drummond in the back with great force. Letting go of Isham, he raised himself up and bent backwards with an awful groan before he collapsed.

My brother and I were paralyzed again, and watched in horror as a grayish figure emerged from behind the great oak tree. His clothes and hat, though ragged and faded, were a uniform we had seen many times before. He was one of our soldiers, and when he briefly turned his head in our direction, we saw a face that was strangely familiar. He first went to Isham, who had slid to the ground, and murmuring something we could not distinctly hear, he leaned over our cousin's motionless form and probed for signs of life.

Picking up a broken tree limb, Matthew scrambled to his feet, and, eluding my second attempt to stop him, he leapt out of the brush.

"Don't you hurt Isham!" he cried, brandishing the limb above his head.

The soldier jumped up and raised his hands.

"I wouldn't hurt him," he said. "He is my cousin."

I knew that voice! Springing to my feet, I ran to Matthew's side.

"Can it be?" I gasped. "Is it Uncle Adam?"

He had a heavy beard now, and long, shaggy hair, but even with these alterations, Matthew and I recognized him in the moonlight.

"We thought you were dead!" my brother marveled.

Our uncle's face worked with emotion for a few moments. All kinds of feelings passed over his features in those few seconds, but it was obvious that his first concern was our poor cousin, and he quickly dropped to his knees at Isham's side as we heard him moan. His eyes fluttered open; he called out for his father, and was stammering and moaning about things we did not understand.

Uncle Adam gently hushed Isham, then looked up at us and said urgently, "I think he is pretty badly hurt. We must take him to the house. There is a wagon nearby, but I think we will get there faster carrying him."

We wondered what on earth a wagon was doing out here, and were about to ask, when we heard our father's voice. He was calling my name. We turned and saw him approaching. Uncle Adam was standing in the shade of the tree created by the moonlight, and as he stepped out of that shade, my father stopped in his tracks. His expression was awestruck, as though he had just witnessed Lazarus emerge from the grave.

Uncle Adam's face contorted with strong emotion, though it was hard to tell if it was sorrow or joy; it seemed to be both.

"Papa, it's Uncle Adam!" exclaimed Matthew, breaking the brief but strained silence. "I told him we thought he was dead—but he isn't!"

Papa lifted his hands and moved forward as if to embrace his brother, but he came to an abrupt stop again when he caught sight of Isham and the dead body beside him. Mr. Drummond had fallen in a twisted position, so that his bloody wound showed plainly beneath the hilt of a Bowie knife. It had hit him squarely in the back, likely severing the spine.

"What's happened?" Papa asked in bewilderment.

Uncle Adam opened his mouth to answer, but Matthew interrupted excitedly.

"Mr. Drummond tried to kill Isham, and Uncle Adam stopped him! You should have seen it, Papa! He was dead before he hit the dirt!"

My father's face was still full of questions, but he could see that Isham needed immediate attention, and quickly scooped him up in his strong arms to bear him back to the house. Matthew and I began following him, but when we looked back, we saw that Uncle Adam was lingering beside the tomb, standing there with his head lowered, and as still as the corpse at his feet.

"Why don't you come with us?" I called out to him.

After a moment he knelt down, pressed one hand against Mr. Drummond's back, and with the other, pulled his knife from the dead man's body. I could see something dark spurt out of the wound; a few drops of blood spattered on Uncle Adam's face, and into his open mouth. He instantly wiped his lips and tongue on his sleeve in revulsion, and then wiped his knife clean on Mr. Drummond's coattail.

"Please, Uncle Adam!" I implored. "You must come inside with us, please!"

There were a few more moments of hesitation, but he finally rose and followed after us. Papa and Matthew were moving quickly, but I lagged behind to be close to my uncle, so close that I could take his rough hand in mine. I saw his lips compress when I did this, and in the darkness, I thought I heard a faint sob.

* * *

Isham was laid atop some quilts on the floor, close

to the fire, and was covered to the chin with a blanket.

Mama cleaned his bloodied head and wrapped it with strips of cotton sheet. She had been as astonished as Papa to see Uncle Adam, but she and everyone else deferred expressions of surprise, curiosity and affection while our wounded cousin demanded all our attention.

"We need a physician," she said to Papa, looking helpless.

"What can a doctor do for him?" Matthew was foolish enough to say aloud.

"Perhaps a great deal," Papa scolded him, and even though he was gazing doubtfully at Isham, who was as pale as death, he went to the door, taking up his hat on the way, and left the house.

Uncle Adam had seated himself on the floor next to our cousin, and picked up his hand. Isham seemed to revive a little with the warmth, and began speaking again in a dazed, gasping manner.

"How my head hurts!" he said. "Oh, Papa! Papa! I didn't tell him!"

Looking very curious, Matthew also took a seat on the floor next to Isham and asked him, "Tell who, Isham? What are you talking about?"

"That man!" he answered. "Papa told me never to tell anyone, and I didn't! Papa said, I must be a good boy—"

His voice trailed off, and he moved his head a little

and gave a cry of pain.

"Don't move, Isham," Uncle Adam urged him gently. "You are a good boy, just as your father said."

Growing more agitated, Isham went on, "I was only to tell Pink, but I couldn't, he was so sick!"

"What were you to tell Pink, Isham?" asked Matthew.

"I can't," he whispered. "I can't"

"You can tell us now," my brother pressed him. "We know all about it now."

Making a gesture to silence Matthew, Mama said it would be better if he remained quiet, and asked us not to speak to him.

"I didn't tell you," Isham said weakly. "Papa and me, only we know what's in the box."

We all exchanged looks of puzzlement, not knowing what to make of what he was saying, but Matthew spoke again, despite Mama's request.

"The box, Isham?" he said. "Do you mean the tomb?"

He opened his mouth to answer, but suddenly gave a shuddering sigh and closed his eyes. The rise and fall of his breathing began to diminish, and Uncle Adam pressed his fingers against Isham's thin wrist to feel for a pulse. In a few moments, we heard the sound of a horse passing the house at a gallop, and Uncle Adam rose, hurried to the door, and called out my father's name.

There was no need for a doctor now.

* * *

An old sideboard table was cleared and moved away from the wall to serve as Isham's resting place that night. We dressed him in his best clothes and laid him out with a single candle burning at his head.

We were all seated at the dining table nearby, and at first our vigil was a quiet one, but after a prayer, Papa turned to his brother questioningly. They were sitting next to each other, and Papa reached out an arm and put it around Uncle Adam, who began to tremble at this gesture of affection, and then suddenly began sobbing. This made my father weep, too, and he put both arms around him.

"Thank god you are alive, Adam," Papa said brokenly. "One we love has been taken from us tonight, but another has been restored."

Still shaking with sobs, Uncle Adam managed to answer, "I tried to save him, but I was too late—too late! I was moving around the big tree to get a better look at the intruder, when I heard Isham cry out."

"We all know you tried to help him," my father said soothingly. "His death is not your fault."

Everyone was anxious to know what had happened, and why Isham now lay dead. Responding to a question from Mama, Matthew told all that he had heard and witnessed that evening.

"But why," she asked, "why was Mr. Drummond trying to open one of the graves?"

Matthew shook his head in puzzlement, but Uncle Adam, who was now more composed, gave an answer.

"After what happened tonight, I think I know. I believe there must be something of value hidden in it," he said. "Isham—"

Interrupting, Matthew suddenly jumped up out of his chair waving his arms wildly.

"It's Uncle Pink's gold!" he shrieked. "It's the gold!"

"Matthew!" Mama said to him reprovingly, glancing in the direction of our dead cousin.

I thought Papa would also reprove my brother for such an unseemly outburst, but instead he looked very thoughtful and after a pause said, "It's very strange, but it comes back to me now...Uncle Pink told me once that my great grandfather was buried under the tomb, and not in it. I had forgotten about that."

"Papa, let's go and see!" Matthew urged him excitedly.

"Well," said my father, looking to Mama. "I suppose we ought to do something with Mr. Drummond, if nothing else."

"I'll help you, Papa," Matthew offered. My father got up from the table and put on his coat again, and Uncle Adam also volunteered to help, informing Papa that he had seen a horse and wagon in the woods that must have belonged to Mr. Drummond.

"To haul off the gold!" Matthew whispered to me.

I insisted on coming along, too, and Papa allowed it.

The four of us trudged back out into the cold night, returning to the cemetery, where all was as we had left it. While Uncle Adam went off to fetch the wagon, Papa picked up the dark lantern, and, finding it still burning, opened its door and held it up to inspect the tomb. He found that one end was partly pushed aside, just wide enough for his hand to pass through. Before he kneeled down and reached in, he peered through the opening by the light of the lantern, and a moment later, he put his hand inside. Matthew and I, standing very close by, soon heard a noise which, though muffled, sounded like very much like the clinking of coins.

Papa pulled his hand out and sank back on his heels. He was breathing heavily. Matthew offered him the metal bar that Mr. Drummond had been using, and with it he pried out the heavy slab of stone even farther. Matthew fell to his knees beside Papa, reached into the tomb, and drew out a canvas bag tied with coarse string. My brother was shaking with excitement.

"Untie it, Matt," said my father.

Matthew placed the bag on the ground, untied the string, and opened it wide to reveal its contents.

"Gold money!" Papa breathed out hoarsely, staggered.

"We're rich, Papa!" Matthew exulted. "We're rich!"

My brother grabbed up the lantern and shone it into the open tomb. I knelt beside him, and over his shoulder I could see numerous identical canvas bags inside. Recovering from his initial shock, Papa fell down on his elbows with clasped hands, thanking God. Matthew jumped up, and, drawing me with him, he took both my hands and swung me around in a frenzied dance of jubilation. He then let me go and danced a jig on his own, laughing and rejoicing. Uncle Adam was just driving up in the wagon, and looked amused by Matthew's antics, though his smile quickly disappeared.

They loaded the dead body into the wagon bed first, and then the canvas bags were carefully placed on board. I counted at least twelve of them, each as heavy and full as the one before.

* * *

Papa covered Mr. Drummond's body with an oilcloth and left it on the wagon which, after being partly unloaded at the house, was taken into the barn.

In the house, we had a large old cedar chest. Its contents, some linens, were removed, and about half the canvas bags were placed inside it. The rest were put into the window seat where Uncle Pink had hidden away his books and papers. When all this was done, everyone gathered at the dining table once again.

Mama was fairly speechless at our good fortune, but Papa could no longer restrain his curiosity about Uncle Adam's surprising and strangely timely reappearance, and he wondered aloud how Mr. Drummond had known about the hidden gold.

Uncle Adam cast his eyes down, and kept them down as he hesitantly offered an answer, as though ashamed.

"I believe Mr. Drummond visited this place before as a soldier," he said. "Last February."

Growing very serious, my father repeated dully, "Last February."

"Yes," said Uncle Adam, adding in a sigh, "I was here, too."

He took a deep breath and went on, "I watched the Yankee soldiers plunder the house, and I saw Drummond, who was then Lieutenant Drummond, wandering about the cemetery with another soldier. Later, at sunset, Drummond returned there alone. I had to hide myself much of the time, and could not see everything he was doing, but I know I saw him at the tomb, studying it very carefully. While I was hiding I heard him doing something, but by the time I looked again, he must have finished. I didn't think much of it at the time, but now I realize he must have opened the tomb and looked inside it that evening."

"He saw the gold!" Matthew exclaimed.

"I think you're right, Matt," said Uncle Adam. "That same evening, some other soldiers joined him in the cemetery. They had found some wine or whiskey in the house, and were somewhat drunk. I heard Drummond tell the other men that he had a mind to dig up some of the graves to see if there was any buried treasure in them, so they fetched shovels and set to digging but, after finding several caskets that held only corpses, they gave up. One of them suggested that they open the tomb to see what it held, but the lieutenant dismissed the idea, pointing at the ivy vines growing up and over its sides, vowing that it had not been opened for a hundred years. I think he must have put back the vines as he had found them before he opened the tomb. 'You will only find another rotting rebel in it,' he said, and they all laughed and returned to the house. They spent the night there and, the next morning, they left taking a wagon load of valuables and household goods with them. As far as I could tell, they did not harm Isham or the few servants who remained, and left them some livestock."

Mama's hand was over her heart as she listened. She shook her head in disbelief and said breathlessly, "So that is why Mr. Drummond came to reside in this neighborhood. He returned for the gold!"

"What a sly dog he was!" declared Matthew.

"Yes, he was sly," Uncle Adam agreed. "He managed to keep the gold a secret known only to himself, and went to the trouble of taking up residence nearby so that his presence and movements would excite no suspicion. Obviously he has been biding his time, waiting for just such a night as this to carry out his plans."

"But how could he know that?" Mama wondered. "How could he know that the gold would still be where he left it, after so many months?"

"I don't think he did know for certain," Uncle Adam replied. "But he had to find out."

"Uncle Pink must have made sure he put those ivy vines back in place when he hid the gold in the tomb," Matthew remarked. "But it's strange that he only told Isham where he had hidden it. Why didn't he tell someone else in the family?"

"Perhaps he told his son Pinckney," said Uncle Adam. "But Pink was very ill when he returned here. The day he arrived, I was watching, and I saw him collapse on the porch. The next day, he was dead. After two of our field hands buried him, they left, and I never saw them again. If Pinckney didn't know, I suppose Isham was to tell him, but he didn't have a chance to do so."

Thinking of our poor dead cousin, I remarked that it was a very wicked man who would murder such a helpless creature for gain.

"But if not for Isham," Matthew speculated, "Mr. Drummond might have gotten away with it—all of Uncle Pink's gold!"

"Yes, perhaps," said Mama, turning her attention to Uncle Adam, whose expression was very somber, "but I believe we also have Adam to thank for our good fortune."

He made no answer to this, and would not look her, or any of us, in the eye. Papa was studying him with a tight-lipped frown, and we all began to feel an uncomfortable tension in the room. My father's voice was tinged with anger when he spoke again.

"What were you doing here in February, Adam?" he asked, adding, "The Yankees did not come into this area until after our troops evacuated Charleston."

"Yes," he answered, in the smallest, lowest voice possible to hear. "I marched out with them, but I did not go farther than this farm."

Papa's face turned hard and wrathful. I had never seen him look at anyone he loved with such coldness.

Uncle Adam kept his eyes lowered and continued, "I lagged behind, and slipped out the ranks, and then I ran into the woods. I have been camped in these woods ever since. I built myself a little hut for the cold weather and rain, just as we did in the army."

With a jaw clenched tightly, my father was taking

deep and deliberate breaths—restraining anger, I could tell.

"You are a deserter," he said after a silence.

Uncle Adam slowly nodded, but then suddenly wailed and covered his face with both hands. When he could speak again, there was still a kind of wail in his voice.

"I was worn out, and ill. I feared the march would kill me, and I knew it was over for us. I knew we had lost the war. We were beaten—beaten!"

He broke down into sobs and bent over the table, still hiding his face.

"You did wrong," my father rebuked him harshly.

"It's true! I did wrong," Uncle Adam groaned. "And I have regretted it and reproached myself every day since. What I did was dishonorable...I gave in to my weakness."

Papa pushed back his chair and rose to his feet. Looking down at his brother sternly, he looked as though he was about to speak, but thought better of it. I was afraid that he would order Uncle Adam out of the house. Mama also rose, looking very distressed, but she too was silent, and followed Papa out of the room.

My brother Matthew, whose expression had been alternating between disappointment and anger as he gazed at our uncle, was the next to leave. I remained at the table, confused, and also disappointed in him, but not angry. I felt sorry for Uncle Adam, though he had committed a very serious offense indeed. He had betrayed our country and our cause. In those times, there were few worse offenses.

Catching his breath to quell the sobs, but still shuddering with emotion, my uncle uncovered his face and lifted his head. When he raised his eyes to mine, they were full of the most abject misery I had ever seen.

"Your father will never forgive me," he said. "None of you will ever forgive me."

"I forgive you, uncle!" I cried tearfully. "From my heart, I do."

I put my hands out across the table, and he took them saying, "You are too good to me, dear little Mattie."

There was a long silence, and to break it I asked him, "Did you know that we all thought you were a ghost?"

"Yes, I hoped that was what everyone would think," Uncle Adam replied. "At first I was hiding myself away because of the Yankees. I had no wish to be a guest again in one of their prisons. Then, after the war was over, I didn't know what to do. There were many times when I simply wished to die. I thought of doing away with myself, but I couldn't bring myself to add a greater sin to the one I had already committed, so I stayed in the woods and keeping an eye on the farm, tried to watch over Isham and the rest. I was so relieved when you and your family came to live here."

"You have been watching us?"

"I've watched you all many hours, Mattie, longing to speak to you, but too ashamed. I must confess to you now that I appropriated some of your chickens from time to time, and I used some of the wood from your fences to build my winter shelter."

"I don't mind that you took the chickens, or the fences," I told him.

"I had just about made up my mind to go away when I saw that Mr. Drummond had come here. I recognized him, and thought it very curious that he had returned, so I decided to stay a little while longer to see what he might be up to."

I wondered why Mr. Drummond waited so long to take the gold for himself. Uncle Adam said that he was a soldier, and had to follow his regiment, and go with his comrades to be mustered out in the north. Later he came back for what he wanted, hoping that it would still be where he had left it.

I told my uncle that Mr. Drummond had purchased timber lands near here, and also that he wanted Papa to go into business with him.

"I doubt that was his real intention," he replied. "But who knows? Perhaps he did mean to settle here and make some money. The gold might not have been there when he returned for it."

Uncle Adam was still holding my hands, and I said to him feelingly, "I'm glad you didn't go away. I wish you would stay with us. You don't know how much we have missed you!"

My uncle tried to smile, but only managed a rueful grimace, and shook his head slowly.

"How can I stay," he said, "when I deserve only your condemnation and contempt...for what I did."

"No, no, Uncle Adam!" I protested fervently. "Did you not serve faithfully for four long years? And you were wounded several times, and nearly died once, and spent months as a prisoner in the hands of the enemy. You were a good soldier! Is all that nothing, because you left the fight just two months before the end of the war?"

"I am a deserter," he replied somberly. "I have dishonored myself and my family...my comrades. I was ill, and my mind was muddled, but that cannot excuse what I did. Oh, Mattie, I would give anything now to change all that, but it can't be undone. I shall go away, and never return."

"No, Uncle Adam, please don't go away!" I begged him.

"It's for the best, Mattie. Better for all of us if I remain dead to you all. If I have no honor, I have no life...so I suppose I am a sort of ghost, after all."

Tears began to roll down my face when he said

this. Uncle Adam was drooping— with sadness and shame, I thought—until he gave a weary groan and leaned over the table, crossing his arms on it and letting his head fall down into his sleeves.

"You must be hungry," I said with concern. "Let me get you something to eat."

"No," he muttered. "I couldn't eat. I must go."

He looked up, turning his eyes toward the door, and I reached over to him and felt his forehead.

"You have a fever, Uncle Adam," I said. "You are ill!"

"Perhaps," he murmured faintly. "I am feeling rather weak now."

"You must stay here tonight. You must not go out into the cold again."

Shaking his head in refusal, he got up from his chair unsteadily, but he heaved a great sigh, supporting himself by placing his hands on the table, and looked as though he could go no further. I ran off to find Papa, and when we returned to the dining room, we found that Uncle Adam had collapsed to the floor.

My father squatted down and picked up his brother in his arms, moving toward the library, where an old sofa awaited him. Uncle Adam was then moved into Matthew's bed after Mama had prepared it. Papa sent me out of the room so that he could undress and bathe him, and when I returned with Matthew, we saw that

Uncle Adam was wearing a clean nightshirt, his head propped up with several pillows. I saw tears streaming down Mama's face as she pulled the covering of a quilt over him, and I grew afraid for him.

"Mama, is he dying?" I asked.

"No, Mattie," she sniffed. "I don't think he is so ill as that."

Papa sent Matthew out to empty the wash basin and bring back some clean water in it. While he was gone, Mama brought a pair of scissors, a straight razor, and a shaving mug into the room and placed them on a table beside the bed.

"His hair and beard are filthy," she remarked.

Papa placed a towel around Uncle Adam's neck, picked up the scissors, and cut his shaggy brown hair and beard very short. Uncle Adam's face was then lathered, and Papa carefully shaved away the remnants of his whiskers. When his face was wiped clean, we were all shocked at what we beheld. There was an ugly reddish scar on each of his cheeks, one of them situated a little closer to his mouth, and the other a little larger and more deformed.

"Was he shot through the face?" Mama asked, wiping away more tears that had sprung into her eyes at the sight of these wounds.

"Clean through," Papa muttered, gazing at his brother's face with dismay.

I saw my father close his eyes, swallow hard, and take a deep breath to gain, or keep, control of himself. He then gathered up the towel and hair clippings and took them out of the room. When he was gone I asked Mama why she had been weeping, if Uncle Adam was not so ill.

"We saw the scars of his wounds as we bathed him, Mattie," she answered sadly. "A gunshot wound in his side...and the terrible scarring of his legs."

"Those wounds on his legs were from a shell that burst near him," Matthew piped up. "It killed the men in front of him! He told us that in one of his letters."

"I remember," said Mama.

She was standing over Uncle Adam, looking down at his face compassionately.

"He is still a handsome young man," she remarked.

I thought he was, too, in spite of his disfigurement, and the dark circles under his eyes. I asked Mama if the scars on his face would heal and go away.

"They will never completely go away," she replied. "But they may look a little better in time."

"Uncle Adam never told us he had been shot in the face," Matthew puzzled. "He never wrote to us about that."

* * *

At daylight the next morning, curiosity and fascination drew my brother back to the family cemetery, to the scene of the awful happenings of the previous night. He went out before breakfast, and a little while later, Matthew returned to the house looking upset. He had been crying, I could tell, though he tried to conceal it.

"I found Wasp," he announced to Mama and me, with a catch in his throat. "Just at the edge of the woods, near the graves. We didn't see him last night. He is dead."

"Poor thing," Mama said feelingly. "Did some animal kill him?"

"I don't think so," Matthew replied. "I think his neck was broken."

"Some man did that," I suggested, sniffing back tears. "Perhaps that man who tried to steal from us."

"Or perhaps Mr. Drummond," said my brother. "I suppose we will never know."

"Poor thing," Mama repeated.

Matthew was about to go and fetch a shovel to bury Wasp, but, hearing stirrings from Adam's room, he followed us there, and we all went in to find that his fever had grown worse. He was delirious, talking excitedly and writhing as if he were suffering from an awful nightmare.

"He's on the battlefield again, Mattie," Matthew whispered to me.

Papa came back into the room when he heard his

brother's voice, and he stood at the end of the bed and watched him with the rest of us for a while.

"Let's go, men!" Uncle Adam cried, throwing his head back and tossing it from side to side. "My god, I am shot! Don't fall back, boys! Forward! Forward!"

He panted, and began raving about an officer.

"Captain Langdon! My captain! Oh, merciful God! The back of his head is shot away! Where is the—where is the—"

Uncle Adam never finished his question. He raised himself up a little from the pillow in a contorted position, but quickly fell back, and after that seemed to sink into a more peaceful unconsciousness.

Papa watched all this silently, and then walked out of the room. A little while later, we heard him bringing up the wagon to the front of the house.

"Your father is taking Mr. Drummond to Charleston," Mama informed us quietly.

Matthew noisily insisted on going with our father, and as Mama quieted him, Papa came into the house. My brother left the table and ran up to him, begging to come along.

"I'm a witness to the crime, Papa!" he said. "I saw everything!"

"So did I!" I exclaimed. "May I come, too?"

"Certainly not!" Papa answered me brusquely, but he told Matthew to go and put on his coat.

Mama rose and came to Papa's side looking concerned.

"Where will you take him?" she asked uneasily. "Not to the military authorities, I hope."

My father shook his head.

"Mr. Drummond was no longer an officer in their army, so I think they have no jurisdiction in this, but I will consult with our cousin Judge Bryant, and see what he advises. It seems to me a matter for our civil authorities."

He glanced into the parlor, where Isham's body lay.

"We mustn't bury him yet. I expect someone will return with me today to investigate what happened here last night."

Mama was wringing her hands anxiously as she watched Papa and Matthew drive off in the wagon. She was very much afraid that he or Uncle Adam might be accused of murder, and treated unjustly. I saw her kneel down and pray for a long time that morning, and as it turned out, her prayers were answered. When the matter was investigated over the next few days, and the facts brought out in a formal inquiry, it was determined that Mr. Drummond's killing was justifiable. During all these proceedings, Papa was careful to reveal only a small amount of the gold which had been his object, to keep the real extent of our fortune a secret.

* * *

We buried poor Isham in the family cemetery, and Papa conducted a funeral service at the grave side. Meanwhile, Uncle Adam was recovering from his illness. His beard began to grow back, and one morning as I sat by his bed, I asked him if he wanted to shave.

"No, Mattie," he said to me gently. "I think I look better with a beard. You can see why, little dear."

I reached out and touched one of the scars on his face.

"Uncle Adam, what caused this?" I asked timidly, fearful that my curiosity might offend him.

"I was shot through the mouth," he replied very matter-of-factly. "We were charging the enemy, and my mouth was wide open with a rebel yell, and good thing, too, for the ball passed through my cheeks and didn't even take any of my teeth or jaw with it. Hit me at just the right angle, I suppose. A friend tied a handkerchief around my face, but I kept bleeding from the mouth, and they took me to a field hospital and fixed me up. It was just a flesh wound, you see, and not so serious as you might think."

My hands automatically went to my cheeks as he described his wound, and I winced and cringed to think of such a thing happening to me.

"It was in the same battle," he went on, reminiscing, "that General Andrews was also shot through the mouth, though he had it much worse than I did. After he was wounded, they put him in an ambulance and brought him to the rear, where I was with the other wounded men. After a while the surgeon came to us and we asked him about the general. He told us that a minie ball had taken off part of his jaw, several of his teeth, and mangled his tongue. After hearing this, I considered myself very fortunate in my wound. They put the general's head in a splint and sent him home, but I heard that though he was deformed, and could only eat soft foods and liquids, he returned to the army the next year."

"You always went back, too, didn't you, Uncle Adam?" I said admiringly. "Each time, after you were wounded, even after you almost died, you went back to the fight."

He lowered his head and eyes and whispered, "Yes, Mattie, I kept fighting, as long as I thought there was hope."

A movement outside the door caught my eye, and I saw Papa walking past. Uncle Adam looked up and saw him, too, sighed, and hung his head again. My father had not come into his brother's room nor spoken to him for days.

"Your father is anxious for me to be on my way," Uncle Adam said, in a tone of dull resignation. "Perhaps I ought to get dressed, and test my strength now."

"Papa has not asked you to leave," I objected.

"He doesn't want me here, Mattie," replied my uncle. "He is ashamed of me. He will shun me for the rest of his life."

"No!" I cried. "None of that is true!"

"Ah, but it is, little dear. I must be going soon."

Papa had burned the remnants of Uncle Adam's uniform, but Mama provided him with a few pieces of old clothes to take its place. He was up and about for a few hours that day, but returned to his bed in the late afternoon, just before Papa and Matthew came in from their work for supper. The next morning, Uncle Adam rose, dressed himself, and humbly asked Mama if she could spare a coat or some sort of covering for him.

"There's no need for you to go outside," she told him, somewhat puzzled.

I was with her, and spoke up to answer for him.

"He wants to leave us, Mama. He says he is not wanted here, and must go."

"You are not well enough yet, Adam," said my kind mother. "And no one has asked you to leave."

* * *

At supper that evening, Mama delicately and carefully brought up the subject of Uncle Adam, relating to Papa his request for a coat.

"He says he must leave," I put in promptly, receiving a look of displeasure from my mother.

Frowning and meditative, my father stared down at the few crumbs of food left on his plate.

"Must he leave, Papa?" Matthew asked, in the meekest tone I had ever heard him use.

After a silence, Papa slowly lifted his eyes to meet my mother's gaze and said, "Adam will have to leave sooner or later. He knows that."

My father sighed deeply, and as he spoke again, there was great pain in his voice and expression—but we soon understood that it had nothing to do with Uncle Adam. Papa had been looking very troubled and preoccupied for days; we thought it was because he was angry with his brother, but now it became evident that something else had been on his mind—Mr. Drummond.

"Think of it—just think of it," he said very slowly and deliberately. "I was seriously considering entering into a business partnership with that man. A thief, and a murderer!"

This was the first time Papa had brought up the subject of Mr. Drummond since he had been cleared of wrongdoing in the man's death.

"The thief cometh not, but to steal and kill," whispered Mama, her voice also strained with emotion.

Papa cast his eyes down at the table again and went on, "I knew it was wrong! From the start, deep in my soul, I knew it was wrong to consider associating myself with him, and yet that day when he rescued

Mattie in the woods, I began to think that it was only my pride that held me back, and that there perhaps was something providential in this man."

"I began to wonder about that, too," my mother confessed. "But you mustn't reproach yourself, dear. You were only tempted because you wished to provide for us."

"I was tempted by more than that," Papa replied, choking, and close to tears.

Seeing Papa in such anguish, Mama rushed over to him and put her arms around him. He immediately rose from the table, and, still embracing, they walked into the parlor. A little while later, as I cleared the table, I could hear my mother and father talking in low, confidential tones, and still later in the evening, when I glanced into the room where they sat, I saw them praying together.

* * *

I found it very difficult to sleep that night. I lay in my bed worrying about Uncle Adam. The night before, I had a suffered a disturbing dream about him, seeing him as a vagabond upon the earth, cursed like Cain of old, wandering and finding no rest, and no friend anywhere. I was afraid the dream would return.

Hours passed, and I was still awake. The house had been very quiet, but suddenly, a cry startled me and brought me bolt upright in the bed. I knew it was Uncle Adam's voice I had heard, and I wrapped myself in a shawl and found my way downstairs. As I entered the hallway, I saw that the door of his room was open. The light of a candle was moving inside, and the next moment, I saw my father walk out.

"Papa!" I whispered.

He turned to me and held up the candle.

"Did Adam wake you, Mattie?" he asked. "It was only a dream, I think—a nightmare, I should say. Go back to bed, dear."

"But you have not been to bed yet, Papa," I replied. He was still dressed in his day clothes.

"I've been reading, and praying," he said, glancing toward the dining room, where I noticed the faint flicker of another candle. "Now you go on up to bed, Mattie."

"I cannot sleep!" I groaned.

Tears sprang into my eyes, and I told him of my distressing dream about Uncle Adam. I tried to describe it, but I broke down, and Papa approached and put his arm around me. He led me into the dining room, sat me down at the table, and took a chair next to me. Laid out in front of him was an open Bible, and beside it, a pamphlet written by a great clergyman Papa admired.

"Mattie," he said, taking my hand. "I think we have raised you to have a proper understanding of things…You are wise enough to know that a man—a man can become too caught up in the things of this world, and forget that it is really not our home."

I was so concerned about Uncle Adam, I don't know that I did really understand my father's meaning at the time, but I listened, and he went on, "When Mr. Drummond offered me a chance at prosperity again, I wanted it badly, so badly that I was half-blinded by my desire, knowing that it was wrong."

"You would never do anything wrong, Papa," I whimpered.

He shook his head and gave a little sigh.

"But Papa, what of Uncle Adam?" I asked tearfully.

"Mattie," he said, "I know you are distressed about the way I have treated him, but you needn't worry about that anymore. I will set things right between us, but it was too hard for me to do that at first. You see, for many months, I have been grieving for my country, and when Adam confessed that he had deserted her, I could not bear it. I shall always grieve for her, Mattie, but I see now that we have not really lost what is most important, for God is with us, and our real country is elsewhere. I can forgive Adam now. How can I do otherwise, when I have been forgiven for the wrong that I have done?"

I was still crying, but my tears were joyful now.

"You will forgive him then, Papa?"

"I will," he said. "I shall speak to him in the morning."

Papa was still holding my hand, and he could feel me shivering in the cold room. The fire had died down to a few glowing sparks among the embers. Blowing out one of the candles, he took the other up again and lit my way upstairs.

After this conversation, I found that I could sleep.

* * *

The following day was Sunday, and Papa surprised us by announcing that we were not going to church that morning. Uncle Adam had just finished his breakfast, and as I removed his tray and dishes and walked out of his room, my father entered and closed the door behind him.

After about an hour, the two men emerged from the bed chamber, and the rest of the day, Uncle Adam spent time with all of us, taking the midday meal and supper with the family. He now seemed fully recovered from his illness, and now that he and father were talking again, Matthew also warmed up to him. My brother, who had been so very disappointed in his uncle at first, now kept close to him as much as possible, and begged to be told his stories of the war.

In the evening, as we all sat together in the parlor, Papa announced that Uncle Adam would be leaving the next morning.

Matthew and I were very surprised and dismayed. Had there not been a reconciliation between the two?

I began to protest, but Uncle Adam gently put his hand on my shoulder to stop me.

"It is for the best, Mattie," he said earnestly. "I know all of you have forgiven me, but this thing I did will always be a black mark against me—and rightly so, but worse than that, it would reflect badly on my family. It will be best for me to go somewhere far away and start afresh—some place where I am not known, where I can begin a new life."

"Where will you go?" asked Matthew. "To Canada? Nannie is there, you know."

"No, not to Canada," my uncle replied with the faintest smile. "Somewhere west, I think—California, perhaps."

* * *

I was so sad to think of Uncle Adam going away that I slept very little that night. When I did sleep, I dreamed that he was traveling in a steamboat, and then in a railroad car, and Matthew and I were with him!

The morning dawned cold but clear, and after breakfast, Papa brought our old carriage up to the house. Mama had provided Uncle Adam with some better clothes, and my father insisted that he take and wear his best overcoat. A valise containing several pieces of clothing and some food was prepared for him, and finally, just before it was time to leave for Charleston, Papa brought out a small share of Uncle Pink's gold and added it to his brother's few worldly possessions.

My uncle was surprised, and made a movement to

refuse the money, but Papa put it into the valise and closed it up.

"I haven't any right to that," said Uncle Adam.

"Uncle Pink would have wished you to have it, and so do I," Papa replied. "This is all you can safely carry with you now, but write to us and let me know when you have need of more."

Heaving one great sob, Uncle Adam threw his arms around my father and embraced him with all his strength, and all the while, Papa held his brother silently and patted his back over and over. Mama was the next person to receive his embrace, and then Matthew, and finally, I reached up and put my arms around his neck. He hugged me, picked me off my feet, and swung me around in the air. I squealed with delight, but the next moment, I began to cry.

"Dear little Mattie," he said fondly, "let's have no more tears. I wish to remember you smiling. I ought not to call you little any more, for you are now a young lady I think, or just about."

I tried to smile, and he gently patted my face.

"You and your brother must write to me, but I shall write to you first to let you know where I am."

Within a few minutes, Mama, Matthew and I were watching Papa and Uncle Adam drive away, keeping our eyes fixed on them until they were out of sight. I had the feeling we might never see Uncle Adam again, but I had come to realize that he was doing the right thing.

In the afternoon, I went out to the kitchen to see old Bess. She was feeling poorly in the cold weather, and was sitting in a sunny spot next to the warm hearth.

"We won't be seeing Uncle Adam anymore," I told her mournfully, stirring up the glowing remnants of the fire with an iron poker.

She nodded, and slowly, a wry smile began to spread across her face.

"Won't be seein' no ghosts, neither," she laughed softly.

Our old cook raised her apron to hide her face in mirthful embarrassment, and I began to laugh and blush, too, feeling a bit foolish, but at the same time, more happy and hopeful than I had for many years.

The following Sunday, Gus came home with us from church, and after a private conversation with my father, he asked me to marry him. I said yes.

* * *

Many years have gone by since these events took place, and with each year my childhood recedes further into what seems more and more a dim, distant past. I have children of my own now, and Gus and I live in a comfortable house in Charleston, next door to the house where I was born and raised, and where Mama and Papa now reside. Uncle Adam settled and married in San Francisco, and my brother Matthew is also married, and helps Papa with his business. My husband, having realized many of his ambitions, looks to fulfill even more in the years ahead. We have been happy together, and I am very proud of him.

At the beginning of my tale, I said you might judge for yourself whether I now give credence to the existence of such things as ghosts, but it is likely you have already guessed that I do not. The mysterious, shadowy being that inhabited our farm was no apparition, no emanation from the grave, but a troubled soul who thought himself lost beyond all redemption in this world, and perhaps the next. No, I do not believe in ghosts, but I do believe in a God of compassion and forgiveness, and in haunted and haunting spirits who sometimes return to the land of the living.

END

ABOUT THE AUTHOR

KAREN STOKES, an archivist with the South Carolina Historical Society in Charleston, S.C., is the author of *Belles, A Carolina Love Story*, a historical novel set in the Civil War South.

She is also the author of *South Carolina Civilians in Sherman's Path*, a non-fiction book released in June 2012 by The History Press, and is the co-editor of *Faith, Valor, and Devotion: The Civil War Letters of William Porcher DuBose*, published by the University of South Carolina Press in 2010.

Also from the Author

FICTION:

Belles: A Carolina Love Story
The Immortals: A Story of Love and War
The Soldier's Ghost: A Tale of Charleston

NON-FICTION:

A Confederate Englishman: The Civil War Letters of Henry Wemyss Feilden (Co-editor)
A Legion of Devils: Sherman in South Carolina
Carolina Love Letters
Confederate South Carolina: True Stories of Civilians, Soldiers and the War
Days of Destruction: Augustine Thomas Smythe and the Civil War Siege of Charleston
Faith, Valor, and Devotion: The Civil War Correspondence of William Porcher DuBose (Co-editor)
The Immortal 600: Surviving Civil War Charleston and Savannah
South Carolina Civilians in Sherman's Path

SOUTHERN LITERATURE is the glory of American culture. Faulkner, O'Connor, Warren, Lytle, Davidson, Gordon, Percy, Chappell, Berry will be known as long as Western civilization survives and long after today's politicians, "experts," and celebrity writers are forgotten. Another of the greats, George Garrett, wrote that "all signs indicate that Southern literature, far from being on its last legs and far from representing a falling off from earlier and better days, seems very much alive." Shotwell Publishing has supported Garrett's witness by launching GREEN ALTAR BOOKS—a collection of Southern fiction and poetry.

For more information on this and other SOUTHERN titles, Please visit us at ShotwellPublishing.com.

From Shotwell Publishing

If you enjoyed this book, perhaps some of our other titles will pique your interest. The following titles are now available at the Kindle Store. Enjoy!

Green Altar Books (Literary Imprint)

A New England Romance & Other SOUTHERN Stories by Randall Ivey

Tiller by James Everett Kibler

GOLD-BUG MYSTERIES (Mystery & Suspense Imprint)

Billie Jo by Michael Andrew Grissom

To Jekyll and Hide by Martin L. Wilson

Splintered: A New Orleans Tale by Brandi Perry

Non-Fiction

A Legion of Devils: Sherman in South Carolina by Karen Stokes

Annals of the Stupid Party: Republicans Before Trump by Clyde N. Wilson (The Wilson Files 2)

Carolina Love Letters by Karen Stokes

Confederaphobia: An American Epidemic by Paul C. Graham

The Devil's Town: Hot Spring During the Gangster Era by Philip Leigh

Dismantling the Republic by Jerry C. Brewer

Dixie Rising: Rules for Rebels by James R. Kennedy

Emancipation Hell: The Tragedy Wrought By Lincoln's Emancipation Proclamation by Kirkpatrick Sale

Lies My Teacher Told Me: The True History of the War for Southern Independence by Clyde N. Wilson

Maryland, My Maryland: The Cultural Cleansing of a Small Southern State by Joyce Bennett.

My Own Darling Wife: Letters From a Confederate Volunteer by John Francis Calhoun. Edited with Introduction by Andrew P. Calhoun, Jr.

Nullification: Reclaiming Consent of the Governed by Clyde N. Wilson (The Wilson Files 2)

The Old South: 50 Essential Books by Clyde N. Wilson (Southern Reader's Guide, vol. I)

Punished with Poverty: The Suffering South by James R. & Walter D. Kennedy

Segregation: Federal Policy or Racism? by John Chodes

Southern Independence. Why War? by Dr. Charles T. Pace

Southerner, Take Your Stand! by John Vinson

Washington's KKK: The Union League During Southern Reconstruction by John Chodes.

When the Yankees Come: Former South Carolina Slaves Remember Sherman's Invasion. Edited with Introduction by Paul C. Graham

The Yankee Problem: An American Dilemma by Clyde N. Wilson (The Wilson Files 1)

FREE BOOK OFFER

Sign-up for new release notification and receive a FREE DOWNLOADABLE EDITION of *Lies My Teacher Told Me: The True History of the War for Southern Independence* by Dr. Clyde N. Wilson by visiting FreeLiesBook.com or by texting the word "Dixie" to 345345. You can always unsubscribe and keep the book, so you've got nothing to lose!

Southern Without Apology.

Made in the USA
Middletown, DE
12 July 2018